AN EYE FOR AN EYE . . .

Seeing a bandit coming from under the stairs with a twelve-gauge riot gun aimed at Ross, McKinney screamed, "Captain!" as he shoved his commander out of the way and tried to bring his weapon up in time. The shotgun roared, and McKinney took the full force of the blast in the gut. The impact propelled him three feet into the air. He died instantly. Ross screamed with rage as he threw his empty weapon down and leaped over the railing and on top of the man with the shotgun, sending them both crashing to the ground. They struggled for a moment, then Ross pulled the shotgun from the man's hands and began smashing the butt of the weapon into the soldier's face until it was nothing but a bloody hole. Grabbing the bag of shells from beside the body, he loaded the shotgun and stepped back out from beneath the stairwell. A Chinese soldier was standing only a few feet from him, his back to Ross; he was raising his rifle to fire when Ross yelled. The startled man turned, and Ross blew the top of his head off . . .

SPECIAL OPERATIONS COMMAND
#2

BURMA STRIKE

JAMES N. PRUITT

BERKLEY BOOKS, NEW YORK

SPECIAL OPERATIONS COMMAND #2: BURMA STRIKE

A Berkley Book / published by arrangement with
the author

PRINTING HISTORY
Berkley edition / November 1990

ISBN: 0-425-12359-6

A BERKLEY BOOK® TM 757,375
Berkley Books are published by The Berkley Publishing Group,
200 Madison Avenue, New York, New York 10016.
The name "Berkley" and the "B" logo
are trademarks belonging to Berkley Publishing Corporation.

PRINTED IN THE UNITED STATES OF AMERICA

10 9 8 7 6 5 4 3 2 1

These books are dedicated to the silent heroes of Special Operations Command, whose dedication to duty and commitment to excellence in defense of the oppressed will one day be appreciated by freedom-loving people everywhere.

To my loving wife, Charlotte, who stood by me through twenty years of battles, not only in war, but in peace as well. To my son, Airman Jason W. Pruitt, who matured beyond his years under the guidance of a part-time father who could not be any prouder. For my daughter, Angela, who has forgiven me for missing so many of her school activities in order to write these books. Last, but far from least, to Jim Morris, my editor and friend, without whose kind and understanding support I could not accomplish this work I love so much.

CHAPTER *1*

B. J. Mattson moved his six-foot-four, two-hundred-pound frame with remarkable speed as he sidestepped the low kick and thrust and executed a snap block to the pressure point on the side of his attacker's wrist. He followed the block with a left-hand jab and a right butt strike to the ribs. The blows brought a grunt and a low moan from his victim who now staggered back and managed to cross block Mattson's tip strike to the temple.

The attacker reached behind his back and brought forth a knife. Stepping forward, he attempted a downward stab. B.J. stopped the attack with a high inside block, followed with a left hand grab of the knife-wielding wrist, while at the same time delivering a heel strike to the back of the attacker's knee. He finished him off with a spinning left foot sweep that dropped the man flat on his back with such force that the others in the gym stopped what they were doing and stared in B.J.'s direction.

"Goddamn, B.J.," said Jake Mortimer, as he pushed himself up on one elbow and smiled. "We've got to get you laid, partner. Ever since Charlotte left, you've got too damn much energy built up in that old worn-out body of yours."

Mattson returned the smile as he leaned forward and extended his hand to Mortimer, "Old body my ass. I'd say this ol' Army bod' made quick SEAL meat out of you, Navy Commander."

Jake reached up and grabbed B.J.'s hand.

"Yeah. I guess you're right."

Tightening his grip on Mattson's hand, Jake suddenly brought his right foot up, jerking B.J. forward. At the same time, he placed his foot in the pit of Mattson's stomach and rocked back with all his might, flipping the army major up and over him. Mattson slammed down hard on his back behind Jake. The sound of the impact brought a low muttering of imagined pain from the observers around them.

Jake rolled over on his stomach and propped himself up on his elbows; he stared at a stunned B.J. who lay perfectly still, eyes open, staring up at the rafters in the ceiling and mumbling curses.

"Smarts a little, doesn't it?" said Jake.

B.J. was silent for a moment, then broke out in a laugh as he rolled over on his elbows and winked at the thirty-one-year-old lieutenant commander with the light blond hair and deep sky blue eyes who had become his partner only two short months ago. "No, Jake. It smarts *a little* on you young shits! It hurts like hell on us *old* fucks."

Jake laughed. The small dimple on his left cheek highlighted the former SEAL commander's grin as he said, "What do you think? Figure two hours of this Tae Kwon Do business is enough to make us the most feared men in world?"

Jumping to his feet, B.J. stretched and twisted slightly to one side working out the kinks in his back muscles as he replied, "Yeah. But I wouldn't count on Chuck Norris losing a lot of sleep over it."

Jake pushed himself up on his knees. B.J. was still grinning as he reached his hand out to help his partner up. Mortimer started to reach for it, but quickly pulled his hand back. "Oh no, you don't."

"Jake! I'm surprised at you. You don't think I'd try anything underhanded do you?"

Springing to his feet, Mortimer slapped Mattson on the back. "Of course not, partner. But I couldn't see spending thirty minutes meditating the yin and yang of the problem."

"Well, let's yin-yang our way over to the club and have a drink while we contemplate the mysteries of the universe."

"Now that's the true art of consciously altering the state of mind. Let's go," answered Jake.

The two SOCOM officers walked into the MacDill Air Force Base Officers' Club. It was Saturday afternoon and business was slow. A life-sized poster board stood at the entrance that led to the stag bar. The attractive lady in the gold spangled dress on the poster was Connie Francis, who was scheduled to give two performances at the club's main ballroom that evening.

"She's still one hell of an attractive gal," remarked B.J. as they stood admiring the cutout.

"You got that right. I guess she finally found out where the boys are," laughed Jake, as he patted the rear-end portion of the cutout and they walked into the dimly lighted stag bar.

Sheri Collins, the long-haired blonde bartender waved to them as they seated themselves in plush captain's chairs at the far end of the bar.

Sheri came up to them. Her striking blue eyes fixed solely on Jake as she smiled and in a sultry tone said, "Hi, Jake. What would you like?"

Jake melted the poor girl in her shoes as he flashed the pearly whites and the dimpled smile.

"Sheri, you're beautiful as always. Scotch and water, please."

Sheri's eyes seemed to sparkle in her smoothly tanned face. She was a junior at the University of Tampa and worked weekends at the MacDill Officers' Club. Not only was she built like the proverbial brick shit house, but she could fix the best drinks in Tampa as well. To say she was infatuated with Lieutenant Commander Jake Mortimer would be a gross understatement.

"Anything—else?" she whispered in a low, provocative voice.

Jake shifted slightly in his chair. This vibrant hunk of

woman was beginning to get to him. She had only been working here one month and in that time she had been hit on by practically every officer on the base. Everyone but Jake, that is. He always had a smile for her and maintained the proper attitude expected of an officer when in the presence of a lady, but he never asked her to go out with him. Not that he hadn't thought about it more than once. Sheri Collins looked like a stack of dynamite on a short fuse. He could just imagine how lethal that body would be without clothes. He'd thought about it, but there was this age thing that kept popping into his mind. She was ten years younger than Jake, and he was already beginning to get a reputation as a ladies' man, but at least those ladies were closer to his own age. This would be more like robbing the cradle. Squaring her shoulders and thrusting a perfectly shaped thirty-six-inch chest right in Jake's face, she whispered, "You sure you wouldn't like anything else, Jake?"

Five years of the age difference had just disappeared. The slow left to right motion of a slightly extended tongue across full lips wiped out another three years. The sexy, promising eyes that were now locked with his closed the generation cap completely.

"Well, yes, there is one other thing, Sheri. Would you like to go out tonight?"

Sheri's face beamed as she answered, "I'd love to. I get off at ten. Is that too late?"

"Not at all. I'll make reservations at Malio's. We'll have a late dinner and a couple of drinks, then we'll take a walk along the beach, okay?"

"Sounds wonderful, Jake. I'll get your drink now," she said as she twirled on her heel and headed back down the bar.

"Uh—Excuse me!" said B.J. "I hate to interrupt this moving, yet very touching love scene, but do you think I might possibly get a Jack Daniel's on the rocks before you two go tiptoeing through the sand?"

Sheri blushed as she cried, "Oh, B.J., I'm sorry. Of course, one Jack on the rocks and one scotch and water coming up."

As Sheri busied herself with the drinks, Mattson lowered his head and swung it slowly from side to side.

"What's your problem, B.J.?" asked Jake.

"Man, if a certain redheaded airline hostess we know finds out you've been shifting sands on the beach with that little girl, you're going to wish you had a hundred more hours of that Tae Kwon Do."

"Karen? You're wrong. She was transferred to the west coast route. Packed it up and left three days ago. I'm really going to miss her. We had some great times together."

"Not one for long periods of mourning, are you partner?" laughed B.J. as Sheri came back. Setting their drinks in front of them, she winked at Jake and left.

Major Erin Hatch, the SOCOM G-2 Intell Officer, came into the bar. Spying the two in captain's chairs, he walked up behind them and placed a hand on each man's shoulder.

"Well, well, if it isn't the M&M boys. How's it going fellows?"

Mattson pointed to the chair next to him as he answered, "Fine, Erin, have a seat, but, please, no more of that M&M shit. Okay?"

Hatch laughed as he slid into the chair and called to Sheri for a Jack and Coke. Jake leaned forward and asked, "Hey, Major, just how did this M&M business get started anyway?"

"Quite by accident, really. When you boys got in that shit down in Ecuador a couple of months ago, one of our radio operators here noticed your names come across on a Teletype message from the embassy. The operator on that end must have figured he could shorten his traffic by eliminating the full spelling of Mattson and Mortimer, so he just inserted M&M. Our boys in SigCom thought that was pretty cool and picked up on it. Next thing you know, the one-liners started popping up all over the place. Stuff like, M&M, they don't melt in your hand, they melt all over you, M&M, Mangle and Mayhem, and the one most people liked was the advanced physics and mathematical term, M&M squared equal TNT. Yes sir, some little ol' radio operator down south has made you boys famous. Hell, who knows?

Before long they might even start putting your mugs on those silk-screened T-shirts."

Mattson downed a hefty shot of his drink and glanced over at Mortimer.

"Better lift your feet, partner. The shit's getting pretty deep."

"Okay, okay," said Hatch. "No more M&M jokes. But seriously, you two guys pulled off one hell of a job down there and everybody knows it. Thanks to you, General Johnson was able to swing the appropriation request for the funding of the new high tech communications gear and the night vision equipment we've been needing. God, the brass from the other services were squealing like stuck pigs over that—in private of course. What could they say? You exposed a crooked finance minister, a power-crazed general who murdered his own men, and a corrupt province governor who procured little girls for a sex pervert. Add to that the fact that you rescued a close and personal friend of the president of the United States. Now I ask you, what member of the National Security Agency or the Joint Chiefs of Staff would publicly criticize that? Not a damn one. You can bet your ass."

Mattson sat silently, turning his glass slowly on the bar. Without looking up, he softly said, "Yeah, Erin, but it cost us a hell of a lot."

Hatch stared down at his drink as Jake muttered, "Amen, brother."

On the downside, the Ecuadorian mission had been costly indeed. Of the two twelve-man "A-Teams" deployed from Panama, eleven had been killed and five wounded. Included among the dead had been an old friend of B. J. Mattson. Sergeant Major Kenny McMillan had arrived with the two teams. He didn't have to come along, but B.J. had requested that he accompany them. Now he was dead. The Navy's SEAL Team Five had lost their commander and suffered two wounded in the rescue of the consul general. All in all, an increase in appropriations funding didn't seem like a fair trade. It never did.

On the upside, they proved that, given the opportunity to

work unimpeded by interservice bickering, bureaucratic red tape, and political interference, Special Operations could accomplish any mission they were given.

"Hey, fellows, are you ready for another round?" asked the sparkling-eyed Sheri.

The morbid feeling of only a moment ago subsided as all three officers looked up at the blonde beauty's gentle face. Hatch pulled two twenty dollar bills from his billfold and tossed them on the bar. "Set'em up all around, sweetheart, and let me know when that runs out."

Sheri smiled as she gathered up the glasses. "Looks like it might get awfully drunk out tonight." Turning to Jake, she searched his eyes for a sign of assurance that their date was still on. He didn't disappoint her as he grinned, then nodded that it was still a go.

"Hey, did you guys hear the one about the poor guy that couldn't get it up whenever he climbed in the sack with his ol' lady?"

B.J. shot Jake a wink as he replied, "Yeah, we heard it from a real good-looking gal just last night. What was that woman's name, Jake?"

"Uh—Hatch, I believe it was. Yeah! She said her name was Jane Hatch. She wouldn't happen to be related to you by any chance would she, Major?"

Erin Hatch's mouth dropped open, then a smile began to break at the corner of his mouth as he said, "Damn! Should have known the bitch was a security risk."

The three were still laughing as Sheri returned with their drinks and departed shaking her head as she thought to herself, "They're rude, crude, and some are even tattooed, but, God, they've got a certain class all their own."

By 1900 hours, business had begun to pick up at the club. B.J. was about to order another round when Major Hatch noticed the time.

"Holy shit! Is that clock right?"

"Sure 'nough," said B.J., as he squinted one eye at the out-of-focus timepiece behind the bar. "Why? You got a date or somethin'?"

Hatch downed his drink and placed a hand on Mattson's

shoulder as he answered, "You might say so. That is, if you call going out with your wife of twenty years a date. She made me promise we'd see both of the Connie Francis shows tonight."

"Big Connie Francis fan from the old days, huh?"

"Naw, not really. But the first time she ever let me in her pants was at a drive-in. They were showing *Where the Boys Are*. Guess you'd call it sort of a *hump* down memory lane. You boys take it easy tonight."

Hatch turned to leave, then paused and looked over at Mortimer.

"Jake, B.J. looks a little out of it. You'd better do the driving tonight. The base commander's death on officers that get nailed with DUI's."

"I have secured his car keys, Major. No problem. Now you better get the hell out of here if you're going to make it back before the first show. Hell, Jane might even let you in those pants again. That is, if you can still get it up."

"Fuck you, Jake," laughed Hatch as he headed for the door.

"No, thanks, I'd prefer to leave that job up to Sheri. But thanks for the offer, big guy."

Hatch was still laughing as he went out the door. Jake turned to say something to his partner and found that B.J. had passed out, head resting on folded arms on the bar. Sheri had seen B.J. waving for more drinks, but given his condition, she thought she had better check to be sure. As she walked up to Jake, she asked, "Is he all right?"

"Just passed out," replied Jake.

There was a hint of concern in her eyes as she said, "I'm not surprised. He's been drinking two to your one. I've never seen B.J. in this condition. Does he do this often?"

Sheri could see the look of concern in Jake's eyes and detected the worry in his voice as he answered.

"No, Sheri. When we came back from down south, his wife had taken the kids and left. He's been hitting the bottle pretty hard since then. I've been meaning to talk to him about it, but these Texas boys are hardheaded, you know."

Sheri seemed surprised. B.J. had been in the club lots of

times by himself over the last two months and had never said a word to her about it.

Jake picked up the money scattered next to Mattson's arm and shoved it into his partner's shirt pocket as Sheri said, "Jake, I didn't know she left him."

"Yeah. I'll tell you about it later."

"Then we're still on for tonight?"

"Jacob Winfield Mortimer never breaks a date with a beautiful woman," said Jake as he maneuvered the major out of the chair. He placed one of B.J.'s arms around his neck and his arm around his partner's waist. Smiling across the bar at Sheri, he reassured her of his return. "I want to see that beautiful face in the moonlight."

The young college girl blushed and giggled, "Jake, that's so sweet."

"Comes across a lot better when you don't have a drunk hanging around your neck. See you at ten. We're out of here."

Jake wasn't in the best shape himself, but somehow he managed to navigate them both out the door of the club and to the parking lot. Unlocking the passenger side door of his car, he tried to lower B.J. into the seat. The combination of three hours of scotch and a healthy dose of fresh Florida air hit him all at once, causing him to lose his balance for a moment. B.J. slid off Jake's shoulder like a wet rag and banged his head against the roof of the car. Somehow, his body defied the natural laws of gravity and fell into the passenger seat. Jake staggered back a step and stared in amazement. He couldn't have put B.J. in that seat any better if he had been stone cold sober. Unlocking his door, Jake slid in behind the wheel, and none too soon. The black Chrysler New Yorker that had just pulled up behind them belonged to SOCOM's number one nemesis, General Raymond Sweet. Sweet was attached to the command, supposedly as a liaison between the Joints Chiefs of Staff and SOCOM. But in actuality the man was a high ranking stooge placed in his position to keep tabs on the unit. Sort of an in-house spy for the wheels in Washington, given the task of causing as much trouble as possible for the Special

Operations Command. Many believed his mission was
solely to instigate situations that would embarrass not only
the unit, but also the United States, in the hope that such
public ridicule would lead to the deactivation of the SO-
COM Command. If his actions during the Ecuadorian crisis
were any example, then the theory was correct. Not only
had he been keeping the SOCOM commander, General J. J.
Johnson, under surveillance, but he had also managed to
bribe a number of the unit's signal personnel to withhold
information from General Johnson during the critical hours
of the Ecuadorian mission. Fortunately, Mattson and Mortimer had wrapped up the mission before the man could do
any damage. An investigation into the affair had resulted in
a massive change of SigCom personnel at the SOCOM
Headquarters at MacDill and 1st SOCOM Headquarters at
Fort Bragg, North Carolina. Sweet had somehow managed
to whitewash his part in the affair. After all, what was the
word of a bunch of sergeants against that of a two-star
general.

Jake adjusted his rearview mirror and slid farther down in
his seat as he watched the short man with the round face and
balding head step from the car and brush his dress blue
uniform a few times with his hand. Jake couldn't shake the
thought that Sweet could pass for the old-time movie star,
Peter Lorre. He could see him in the room with Humphrey
Bogart and Sidney Greenstreet, with the Maltese Falcon
sitting on the table.

An elderly woman with short, silver hair sat on the
passenger side. She was obviously waiting for her husband
to open the door for her.

"One'll get you twenty he won't do it," whispered Jake
to himself.

"Come on, Martha. What are you waiting for?"

"Figures," mused Jake, as he watched the woman climb
out of the car and slam the door in disgust. Sweet didn't
even wait for her to join him. Instead, he turned on his heel
and headed for the club, as if she were supposed to follow
along behind him like the women of Asia, with her head

bowed, keeping a respectable distance behind her provider. This simple action said much about the man himself. As far as Sweet and the men who had sent him here were concerned Special Operations Command was nothing more than an overrated bunch of undisciplined Rambos with a multitude of attitude problems and a disgustingly high opinion of themselves. It was a situation that those in high places intended to do away with at the first opportunity.

Jake waited until Sweet had entered the club before starting the car. Jake and B.J. were high on the man's list of people he most wanted to have thrown out of the military. Their success in Ecuador had made him look like the fool he was, and there was little doubt that he now wanted their heads. B.J.'s continued state of depression and battle with the bottle were becoming the talk of the base. It was certain Sweet had heard the rumors and was simply biding his time, waiting for Mattson to fuck up. This was not a point of conjecture, but one of fact. People who drink in excess to relieve depression succeed only in depressing themselves further. Logic and reason become nonexistent, replaced instead by rage and self-pity. These elements would eventually come together at one time and the results would be bad. Jake knew that B.J. was quickly reaching that point. He couldn't allow that to happen for two reasons: one, B.J. was his friend; and secondly, Sweet was waiting in the wings with a noose in his hands.

Removing the big Texan from the car and getting him to the front door of his house proved to be an exhausting job in itself. Holding him up with one arm, Jake sorted through his keys until he found the one that opened the door. He half-carried, half-pulled Mattson into the living room and lowered him down onto the couch. B.J. muttered something Jake couldn't understand, then curled up in a fetal position and went back to sleep. Finding a blanket in the hallway closet, he returned to the living room and placed it over Mattson. Laying his hand gently on B.J.'s shoulder, he quietly said, "Tomorrow we're going to have a long talk, partner."

Jake stood and switched on the small table lamp at the end of the couch. The light shone down on a gold-framed picture that sat at one corner of the table. It was a picture of Mattson's wife Charlotte and their two kids. She was a beautiful woman. Her long, blonde hair highlighted a soft, smooth face that had maintained the youthful glow of the Texas A & M cheerleader that B.J. had fallen in love with over sixteen years ago. To her right stood Jason, their fourteen-year-old son. He was the spitting image of his father. On the left was Angela, the eleven-year-old daughter, who had been blessed with the same radiant beauty as her mother. The longer Jake stared at the picture, the more he could appreciate the torment his partner was going through. Charlotte had given him a choice: a family or the military. For many people, it would be an easy choice, but this life was all that B.J. had ever known. It was not something that could simply be tossed by the wayside and forgotten.

Jake turned away from the picture, grateful that it was not he who had to make such a decision. He walked into the corridor that led to the front door. While reaching across to switch off the overhead lights, Jake's eyes were drawn to the citation that hung on the wall above the switch. "For heroism in the Republic of Vietnam," Sergeant Bobby J. Mattson had been awarded his country's third highest medal for bravery in combat. Next to that, encased in a black-and-gold frame, hung a bachelor's degree from Texas A & M. Above both of these hung a framed set of orders commissioning ROTC Cadet Bobby J. Mattson to the rank of second lieutenant, United States Army. It was as if B.J. had been living in two separate worlds: one represented by the picture on the table, the other hanging here on the wall. He had now been forced into choosing one world or the other. Jake had no idea which way the situation would go, but one thing he knew for sure: B.J. wasn't going to find the answers in a bottle.

Switching off the lights, he took one last look back at the couch. The dim glow of the table lamp cast its light on his motionless friend, who for tonight was free of all worry.

Closing the door quietly behind him as he left, Jake strolled across the lawn to his car. It was a pleasant Florida night with the stars strewn across a cloudless sky. It was going to be a great night for shifting sand on a secluded beach.

CHAPTER 2

Edward Nickleson, the young freshman congressman from the state of Iowa, smiled at his lovely new bride of only one month as he said, "See, Kathryn, I promised that if you married a politician your life would be one of continuous excitement, and now look where you are. Within an hour we'll be on our way to China, then India, with a final stopover in Thailand thrown in as a bonus. All that in just ten days. Now, how many of the folks back home in Glenwood could even dream of seeing all of those places?"

The twenty-six-year-old farm girl with the long brown hair and large brown eyes stood in awe of the 747 awaiting them beyond the chain link fence. Oblivious to her husband's words as well to the activity around her, Kathryn Nickleson continued to stare at the metal giant. Her feelings ran at two levels: one of wonder, the other of fear. God, she hated flying. The trip from Iowa to Washington had been made bearable only by a handful of pills she had managed to sneak from her grandmother's medicine chest. But that plane had been nothing compared to the monster before her now. There was no mistaking the tension in her voice as she unconsciously took a step back from the cause of her fear.

"Ed—Edward, I—I really think you should make this trip by yourself. I mean, there are still so many things left to do at the apartment. You'll only be gone ten days. That's not so long."

15

"Nonsense, Kathryn. We've only been married a month and with the runoff election and all there wasn't even time for a honeymoon. Senator Kendell was aware of that and was kind enough to call in a few favors to get me placed on his Foreign Relations Committee. He did that, Kathryn, just so we could combine business and our honeymoon all in one trip. How would it look if you backed out now, darling?"

"But, Edward, that thing is so huge."

Wrapping his arms around her trim waist, he pulled her petite, well built body against him and kissed her lightly on the cheek as he asked, "Kathryn, do you trust me?"

Looking up into his light blue eyes, she answered, "Of course, Edward."

"Do you think I would do anything that I thought would harm you?"

Realizing how silly her fears must seem to him, she lowered her head against his chest and whispered, "No, Edward. Of course you wouldn't."

Raising her face in his hands, he winked down at her and smiled.

"Okay, then, believe me when I tell you that once we're on our way, you're going to love every minute of this trip. Just trust me, Kathryn. That's all I ask."

The words were comforting, but did little to untangle a stomach that was twisted in knots. It was not just the size of the plane nor her fear of flying that was bothering her. Somewhere in the back of her mind she could sense that something was trying to warn her away from this place. She couldn't explain it, but it was there and the feeling was strong.

"So what do you say, dear? Are we ready to see the world?"

Managing a modest smile, Kathryn thought of telling her husband about the haunting feelings she was experiencing. But how could she possibly explain something she herself did not understand?

"Edward, I—I—"

"Oh, isn't this just the most exciting thing! I am

practically beside myself with exhilaration. I can't wait till we're in China."

The deep voice so filled with excitement belonged to Wanda Kendell, wife of Senator Charles Kendell. She was an exceptionally tall woman, slightly overweight, with frost-gray hair and the beginnings of a double chin. Patting Kathryn on the arm, she continued, "I think it was just so romantic of dear Charles to arrange for you and Edward to accompany us on this little trip. It will be a honeymoon you will remember for a lifetime, my dear."

Pausing a moment to catch her breath, Mrs. Kendell noticed the pale look on Kathryn's face.

"My dear, you are hardly what one would call the blushing new bride. Are you feeling all right?"

"She has a very hard time with flying, Mrs. Kendell. I believe the size of the plane has her a little concerned," said Edward.

A smile broke through the heavy makeup covering Wanda Kendell's face as she placed an arm around Kathryn's shoulders and spoke in a confident tone. "Oh, darling, there is no need to concern yourself with that. The moment an airline is notified that a Capitol Hill group is going to be flying on one of their planes they spend two days checking everything from the smallest bolt to the spinning action of the toilet roll. I can assure you, Kathryn, that plane out there has been checked over more closely than the day it rolled off the assembly line."

Raising her chubby beringed hand, Wanda Kendell allowed her fingers to slide gently down the side of Kathryn's silky smooth cheek.

"Now, don't you worry about a thing. Once we're on our way, I'll come over and sit with you while the men talk their boring business, okay?"

"Thank you. That's very kind of you."

"Yes. Thank you, Mrs. Kendell." added Edward.

"That's quite all right. I don't mind," Mrs. Kendell replied as she adjusted one of the gaudy bracelets on her wrist and walked away.

"See, darling, there's nothing at all to worry about. She's

right, you know. The last thing in the world a major airline would want would be an incident involving four senators, four congressmen, their wives, and their staff. An investigation would be devastating for them. So, what about it? Are we ready now?"

She lowered her head back on his chest again and in a meek voice said, "I'm sorry, Edward. Please, don't think badly of me."

He tipped her head back and kissed her lightly on the mouth, then took her hand and led her to the escalator that would take them up to the open-air VIP terrace that led to the loading ramp.

As they rode to the top, Kathryn asked, "Edward, I know the trip to China is more or less a diplomatic visit, and the stopover in India deals with economic aid, but why the trip to Bangkok?"

A look of surprise came over Edward's face.

"Why, Kathryn, I'm impressed. I didn't think you had taken the time to read the itinerary."

She returned the smile, happy with herself that she had pleased him.

"I read it yesterday while you were in the shower. But I don't recall seeing any mention of a stop in Thailand."

"You're right, darling. Senator Kendell had to add that one at the last minute. He also serves as a member of the Drug Enforcement Committee. I would imagine the committee chairman requested the stopover. Possibly the president made the request. I'm not sure. But for whatever reason, it will provide us with two fun filled days in the land of the elephants. We'll send your mother a picture of you sitting on top of one of the largest elephants we can find. What do think about that?"

Kathryn Nickleson laughed for the first time since they had arrived at the airport. The haunting feeling was still there, but she chose to ignore it now as she laughed again. She could just imagine the excitement that would be generated by such a picture appearing on the front page of the *Glenwood Bugle*. She would be the talk of the town. She was about to answer her husband when Mrs. Kendell again appeared at their side and resumed her reassurance speech as if she had never left. Edward smiled, then winked at Kathryn as he moved to one wall of the terrace and lit a cigarette, leaving the ladies to their conversation. Replacing the pack of cigarettes in his coat pocket, he rested his arms on the wall and gazed at the bustling activity of one of the busiest airports in the world. Like Kathryn, he often found it hard to believe that he was actually a congressman in the nation's capital.

Edward Nickleson had been persuaded by the local veterans association to run for the office following the sudden and unexpected death of Howard C. Prescott, a kind but elderly man who had maintained his seat in the house for nearly thirty years. Although not a veteran of any foreign war, Edward was the son of a deceased Medal of Honor winner. That was good enough as far as the VFW was concerned. They were a strong force in the region and had the funds, as well as the backing to launch an effective campaign for the thirty-two-year-old lawyer and son of a hero. Their campaign had been built on strong patriotism and the need for more youthful and energetic blood to represent the state of Iowa in the House. It had been one of the most lopsided elections in the state's history with Nickleson drawing ninety-three per cent of the vote.

It is amazing how things work out, thought Nickleson to himself as he inhaled deeply on his cigarette and watched a luggage cart snake its way from a tunnel beneath the terminal to stop at the loading compartment of their plane. Two men in coveralls began tossing suitcases and bags to two other men positioned in the open cargo bay. Taking a final puff of his cigarette, Nickleson dropped it over the wall. As he was turning to leave, his attention was drawn to the sudden appearance of three men just exiting the tunnel below. Stepping back to the wall, he recognized the man in the middle as Senator Kendell. He was flanked by two large, burly men dressed in black business suits, who each carried a large brown suitcase. As the trio approached the baggage cart, Senator Kendell stepped forward and spoke with the man in charge for a brief moment, then waved his two friends forward. Unlike the previous loading procedure, these bags were not simply thrown aboard, but were passed carefully up to the bay loaders who waited until one of the men in black climbed up into the cargo bay and disappeared inside, returning only when both bags had been personally loaded and secured. Satisfied that all was in order, the three men then moved to the escalator that would carry them up to the loading terrace.

Nickleson watched as the cargo bay door was shut and secured, and the cart pulled away. Even though he was new at this congressional business, he found it odd that a senior senator would personally concern himself with the loading of luggage. But then this was Washington, D.C. and Washington was an oddity in itself, a fact that the young congressman had discovered upon his arrival in the capital to be sworn in.

Within twenty-four hours after officially becoming a junior member of the Washington elite, he had been counseled on the ground rules that applied to his new position. Personal appearance was to be maintained at the highest level at all times, especially in public. He was to make a point of appearing at any and all charitable functions, if possible, particularly those covered by the media. When asked a question by a reporter or newscaster, he was to always give both the pro and con side of the question, thus avoiding a direct answer one way or the other. Finally, he never, for any reason, was to contradict a statement or the actions taken by the party's majority leader. In this case, that was Senator Kendell. Such behavior was unacceptable at any time.

That was the public image he had to maintain. His private activities, however, be they extramarital affairs, homosexuality, drugs, or the swinging life-style, were all perfectly acceptable as long as they were conducted with discretion and out of the public eye. Senator Kendell had provided him with a list of phone numbers that he could call if he should ever be discovered while involved in any of those private activities. There were no names on the list, only numbers. He only had to explain the situation to the voice on the other end of the line and the problem would be discreetly handled for him—no muss, no fuss. He was a congressman now. He could do just about anything he wanted. He had laughed jokingly when Kendell had presented him with the list and explained its meaning. He assured the senator that he and Kathryn were perfectly happy, and there would be no need for such numbers. Kendell had only smiled, placed the list in Nickleson's pocket, and made the remark that that was what all new arrivals said at first, but in his twenty-four years on the Hill, he could not recall the name of one elected official who had not found it necessary to utilize the list of numbers at least once. Nickleson kept the numbers.

Kendell was flanked by the two men in black as the trio stepped from the escalator. They were both taller than the senator and weighed well over two hundred pounds each. Kendell was far from small, himself. He stood six feet and had managed to maintain a youthful physique, with broad shoulders that tapered down to a thin waist. It was hardly the body one would expect of a man near sixty. His salt-and-pepper hair was neatly trimmed and his blue-green eyes stood out in a dignified, square-jawed face. The three walked up to Nickleson.

"Well, Edward, are the honeymooners ready to begin their world tour?" asked Kendell in his distinct Southern drawl.

Nickleson smiled, but was not totally comfortable with the two men who now stood behind and slightly to the right of the senator. At first he thought they were Secret Service, but up close, he disregarded that theory. The clothes were right but not the personal appearance. Secret Service operatives prided themselves on their impeccable neatness and appearance. Their hair was always neatly cut and maintained, the occasional mustache was well kept. They all seemed to have that smooth, unblemished face that identified them as the all-American boy. Neither of the men in black fit that description. Their hair hung down around their ears. The one on the left had a narrow white scar that ran from just behind his left ear, down the cheek and along the neck, disappearing beneath the starched white collar of his button-down shirt. The man on his right had a small pencil mustache and a badly acne-scarred area below his right eye. Nickleson could feel their penetrating eyes staring at him from behind their dark sunglasses. They made him nervous.

Senator Charles Kendell was aware of the young congressman's nervousness as he studied his two associates.

"Goddamn, where are my manners? Edward, let me introduce you to my friends here." Gesturing to the taller of the two men he continued, "This is Mr. Alfonso and the other gentleman is Mr. Rivera. They are employees of a private security firm that I utilize when I go on these trips."

Raising his hand quickly in Nickleson's direction, he laughed as he said, "Now, before you ask, I want you to know that I pay for this service myself—not the taxpayer."

"Of course, sir." Nickleson had blurted out the reply before he even realized it. "Are you expecting some sort of trouble on this trip, Senator?"

"No, No. Nothing like that Edward. But with the world situation being what it is today, let's just say, an ounce of prevention and all that, you know. It's only a precaution. Nothing to worry about, I assure you. Now, let me see if I can drag that wife of mine away before she talks poor Kathryn's ear off. We'll talk later, Edward."

Nickleson caught a glimpse of a pistol grip in a shoulder holster under Mr. Rivera's coat as the three men turned and walked away. It only added to the uneasy feeling he had about the two men. Kathryn came up to him and slid her arm around his.

"I certainly won't be lacking for conversation on this flight, darling. Mrs. Kendell was about to give me the history of the great state of Georgia when the senator rescued me. She's a nice lady, but my word, she loves to talk."

Nickleson's eyes were still fixed on the men in black. He had heard only part of what his wife had said.

"What—what was that Kathryn?"

Staring up at his troubled eyes she asked, "Edward, is there something wrong?"

"No, honey. My mind was on something else. I'm sorry. We had better go. They'll be loading in a few minutes."

Holding hands, they began the short walk to the loading area. Kathryn suddenly stopped. A look of panic came over her face.

"Oh, Edward. I just had a terrible thought."

"Now, Kathryn, I thought we had this aircraft fright business taken care of."

"It's not that, Edward. Do you remember telling me to pick up a gift to present to our host in China?"

"Yes, I do. Did you forget, Kathryn?"

"No, but you may wish I had. I had no idea what to buy, so one of the salespeople suggested a lighter. I found one that I thought would be appropriate. Oh, Edward, the thing looks like a gun. You pull the trigger and the end of the barrel lights up. I never thought— I'm so sorry. The airport security people will probably be coming up to arrest us at any minute now."

Nickleson stopped walking. Wrapping his arms around her, he tilted her small, beautiful face up to his and grinned as he said, "Oh, Kathryn, I love you. There is so much for you to learn."

"But they'll think it's a real gun, Edward."

"Darling, I'm a congressman now. We have political exemption from luggage and custom searches anywhere in the world. Now stop worrying and relax. This is supposed to be our honeymoon, remember."

Kathryn smiled and hugged his strong arm against her breast.

"Thank you, darling. I promise you, I'll get better at this." They continued onto the loading area, arriving just as the stewardess began taking the tickets. Wanda Kendell had been right about one thing, the Nicklesons were about to embark on the trip of a lifetime. For some, it would be their last.

CHAPTER 3

The hard rubber ball came off the wall like a stray bullet. Jake Mortimer scrambled across the court, catapulting his six-foot-two frame horizontally into the air and giving the ball his best backhand shot before he slammed onto the hardwood floor. The ball caught the edge of the graphite racket and ricocheted into the corner behind him.

"That's point and game, Commander," said General J. J. Johnson as he recovered the ball, grabbed up a towel from the corner, and mopped the sweat from his face.

An exhausted moan came from Mortimer as he rolled over on the cool floor of the racquetball court. He glanced up at the white-haired, fifty-nine-year-old commander of SOCOM who had just whipped his ass in three straight matches and tried to figure out where the old man found all that energy.

"Not going soft on me are you, Commander?" asked Johnson as he walked up to the outstretched body and dropped a towel onto the navy SEAL's sweat covered face.

Pulling himself up into a sitting position, Jake wiped the sweat from his face and grinned up at his boss. "Guess I just overdid the extracurricular activity over the weekend, sir."

"Yeah, that's what I've heard," smiled Johnson.

Jake seemed surprised and a little bewildered by the general's reply.

"Excuse me, sir, but just what—?"

"Sheri, isn't it? The young college girl with blonde hair and a great ass that works at the O. Club on weekends."

"Why—yes, sir. But how?—I mean, who—?"

The general was smiling a fatherly grin as he answered, "It would appear that your moral character has been judged inappropriate for that of an officer and a gentleman, Commander."

"By whom, if I may ask, sir?"

"The forthright and dignified ladies of the MacDill Officers' Association. A rather lofty group that is headed by none other than the wife of our chief pain in the ass, General Sweet. It seems that Mrs. Sweet and the ladies feel you are taking unfair advantage of the young Collins girl. Or so they said at seven o'clock this morning."

Jake wadded up the towel and threw it across the court in disgust.

"They called you at seven this morning about this?"

"Yes they did, Jake. Mrs. Sweet was very apologetic about the hour but thought I should be made aware of the situation so that I might take appropriate action to protect the young lady's virtue." Johnson paused a moment, struggling to maintain a straight face. He continued, "I thought about reminding her of that old saying about shutting the gate after the horse was out, but thought better of it. Mr. Mortimer, I am an officer and a gentleman; therefore, I will not inquire as to your activities over the past weekend, nor to the subject of the young lady's virtue remaining intact. Having found myself in your present situation on more than one occasion, I believe I already know the answer to that."

Jake's face took on the appearance of a little boy caught with his hand in the cookie jar.

"Uh—sir. I swear to God, I only acted in self-defense. One minute we were kissing and then, wham! Next thing I know she flips me on the sand and—then—then—" Jake lowered his head. Trying desperately to suppress a laugh, he spoke in an embarrassed whisper. "Oh, the shame of it, sir, I—I was date raped."

General Johnson could no longer contain himself as Jake

broke out in a mock fit of crying. Laughing, he reached out his hand and helped the Navy commander to his feet.

"That's one hell of an alibi, mister. I think I'll spare the Ladies' Club all the gory details and just inform them that we had a discussion on the matter, okay?"

"You're the general, General," laughed Jake.

After showering and storing their equipment, Johnson suggested a late lunch at the Officers' Club.

The dining area was practically empty of the noonday crowd as they found a table in the corner. The waitress brought them menus and coffee, then departed. Stirring a packet of sugar into his coffee, Johnson's eyes remained on the swirling coffee as he said, "Jake, tell me what has been happening with Major Mattson."

Mortimer glanced at the general over his uplifted coffee cup.

"I'm not quite sure what you mean, sir."

The old man's eyes were locked onto Jake now. "Let's skip the bullshit, Commander. B.J.'s been on the bottle ever since you both came back from Ecuador. It is also my understanding that you had to carry him out of here Saturday night. Now is that right, or did I happen to get some piss poor information?"

Lowering his coffee cup, Jake shifted in his chair.

"No, sir, your intell was correct. B.J. is having a problem adjusting to his present situation. I'm sure that you're aware that his wife took the kids and left just before we came back."

Johnson nodded that he was familiar with the marital situation.

"General, that's really the problem. He's been backed into a corner where he has to choose between a wife and family or the military. The major is having a hard time dealing with that, sir."

"I see," said Johnson. "Of course you realize that he won't find any answers in the bottom of a bottle, Commander."

"Of course, sir," replied Jake as he stared down at the

table and pushed a fork aimlessly around on the tablecloth. "I'm sure B.J. is aware of that, too, sir. But for right now, the booze seems to help. Gives him more time to sort it out, I suppose."

A frown etched its way along the general's forehead as he continued to stare across the table. There was a firmness in his voice as he said, "I will remind you, Commander, that alcohol is one of the most addictive substances there is when you have problems. Unfortunately, I've watched more than my share of damn good officers lose everything because they needed a few drinks to sort things out, as you say. I know what I'm talking about here, Jake. When my son was killed in Grenada, I did plenty of sorting out. Major Mattson is a hell of an officer. I can't say what he'll decide to do in this situation, but whatever he decides, I want it to be his choice, not the bottle's. You get my drift, Jake?"

"I'm his friend as well as his running partner, sir. I won't let things go that far. You can count on that."

General Johnson nodded his approval of Jake's promise as the waitress brought their lunch to the table. For the next thirty minutes they ate and discussed SOCOM and ladies' clubs. Finished with his meal, Johnson leaned back in his chair. Ignoring the no smoking sign on the wall behind Jake, he lit up a cigar. Watching the blue-white smoke curl its way upward, he asked, "Jake, tell me something. Why would a man with a law degree from Harvard who comes from one of the most prominent families in Philadelphia want to risk his ass running around the world chasing down terrorists, drug dealers, and all the other scum of the earth?"

Jake flashed the dimpled smile as he looked over at the general.

"If you ask my grandmother that question, sir, she would tell you it was the result of playing football at Harvard. Grandmama is convinced that her favorite grandson suffered substantial brain damage from too many hits on the head while performing the duties of a running back at that illustrious institution."

"Do tell," laughed Johnson as he took another puff.

"She's really a wonderful old gal, sir. You'd like her. But

to answer your question, I guess I was always considered the wild one of the bunch. Never could take things as seriously as my brothers or my sister. Special tutors and hours and hours of study, followed by more hours of worrying over grades and status on honor rolls and all that bullshit. It just never concerned me that much. I'd go to class, listen to the lectures, take a few notes, then go on about my business. Seems I had something the others didn't: total recall. Used to really piss my brothers off. They'd study for weeks while I went to parties almost every night, but I'd always score higher than they did on the tests. Hell, I always figured school was supposed to be fun, so I had fun and maintained a respectable grade point average at the same time. The closer it came to graduation, the more I realized that I didn't want to be stuck behind a desk in some office on the eighteenth floor of my daddy's law firm. So, being the rebel of the Mortimer clan, I did what any respectable rebel would do. I joined the Navy. Mom cried, Dad cussed, my brothers were overjoyed, and Grandmama recommended a good neurosurgeon. My grades and my father's name helped secure me commission. That was ten years ago, sir. I can honestly say there has only been one occasion when I considered resigning my commission, and that was when I was notified that I was to be transferred to this command."

General Johnson stared across at the thirty-one-year-old Navy man, a look of surprise on his face, "I was not aware of that, Commander. Could you tell me why?"

"It was nothing personal, sir. But after SEAL training and running operations with the Delta Force as a SEAL Team commander, I found it ironic that I was about to be assigned to the very thing I had tried to avoid ten years ago. I had visions of an office and a paper-shuffling desk job waiting for me here at SOCOM. It wasn't a very pleasant thought, sir."

"Well, considering that within twenty-four hours after your arrival I linked you up with a major that you didn't know, placed you in a position on my staff that officially doesn't exist, then sent you to a country where a substantial number of people were attempting to kill you, that's not quite the normal office and desk work one would expect of a headquarters. Now that you've been with us a few months, what is your opinion, Jake?" asked Johnson.

"I wouldn't want to be anywhere else, sir," smiled Mortimer.

Tapping the ashes from his cigar onto a napkin next to his coffee cup, Johnson replied, "Very good, Commander. I like my people to be happy in their work. Now what are we going to do about Major Mattson? General Sweet would love nothing better than to nail him to a cross for alcohol abuse and conduct unbecoming an officer. I won't lie to you Jake. If B.J. screws up while under the influence of alcohol, there isn't a hell of a lot I can do for him. The brass is really cracking down, especially with officers."

"Yes, sir, I know. I just missed running into General Sweet in the parking lot the night I took B.J. home. MacDill is not exactly what one would call a vast military reservation. I'm afraid it will be just a matter of time before Sweet and Mattson run into each other one night, and if B.J.'s been on the booze, that'll be the end of it."

General Johnson sat quietly for a few moments, deep in thought. His eyes seemed to light up as he leaned forward and a smile spread across his face. "You have a good point, Jake. We need to get you boys away from the flagpole for a while. There's another old saying: "Out of sight, out of mind." Besides, it can't be doing B.J. any good having to go home to that empty house every night. I think it's time you both took a little trip. What do you think?"

Jake sat back in his chair and stared across at the cotton-topped head of the man fondly known as Q-Tip. The weathered lines on the general's distinguished face were not solely from age, but rather had been acquired over a period of nearly thirty years of flying combat missions in Korea, Vietnam, Grenada, and countless other places around the world. They were lines forged by being a troop commander, not a desk commander like so many of those who now ruled in high positions. Johnson had spent his time on the ground, seen his share of death and killing, and experienced the fear of staring into the face of the grim reaper on more than one occasion. He was one of those rare officers who, no matter how high in rank or status he might go, would always have time for the men under him. His concern for B.J. was a perfect example. How many other officers, let alone generals, would even bother?

"What did you have in mind, sir?"

Removing the cigar from his lips and crushing it out on a saucer, he answered, "How would three weeks in Thailand set with you boys?"

Jake Mortimer's mouth dropped open. Thailand! Every soldier's dream assignment. Asian beauties with long, black hair, skin as soft as a baby's butt, and eyes that could tempt the Pope himself.

"Thailand, sir, for three entire weeks? Who do we have to kill, sir?"

Johnson laughed as he leaned forward, "No one, Commander. SOCOM has one company of the 75th Rangers departing Fort Lewis, Washington at midnight tonight. They will be conducting a joint training exercise with the Royal Thai Special Forces beginning four days from now. It will be a three-week exercise and since it involves a foreign government, I see nothing wrong with sending two of my top-notch advisers to evaluate the training. You think B.J. might be interested?"

"If he isn't, sir, I have the name of an excellent neurosurgeon. When could we leave?"

The general could hear the excitement in Jake's voice.

"We can have the orders cut this evening, get you both paid by the finance officer first thing in the morning, and on a plane for Fort Lewis by this time tomorrow afternoon. You'll lay over at Lewis for a briefing on the exercise from the S-2, then leave for Thailand the following day. How does that sound, Jake?"

Smiling and resting his elbows on the table, Jake replied, "General, in my ten years in this business I must say with all honesty that that is without a doubt one of the most concise movement orders I've ever heard. Simply fucking outstanding."

The waitress had approached the table just as Jake had finished. She now stood stone-still, her face registering both shock and disgust that an officer would use such language, especially in the presence of a general. Jake glanced up, then quickly away, momentarily embarrassed.

Johnson shook his head and laughed. Looking up at the waitress, he tried to keep a straight face as he said, "You'll have to excuse the commander. He was raped by a blonde over the weekend, and the poor boy hasn't recovered from it yet."

The stunned woman let the bill drop from her hand to the table, then with scolding eyes stared down at the general as she said, "I would have expected more from you, sir."

Johnson burst out in a loud uncontrollable laugh as he replied, "That's exactly what that blonde said to him after it was over."

The general returned to headquarters to get started on their orders while Jake headed for Mattson's quarters to inform him of the pending mission. As Jake stepped from his car, he noticed that all the blinds were closed. An overflow of mail was sticking out of the mailbox and rolled newspapers littered the yard. If he didn't know any better, he would have thought no one was home, but B.J.'s car was in the garage with the driver's side door open. Shattered glass from a broken whiskey bottle lay scattered in front of the side door that led into the house from the garage. Jake knew his partner was rapidly approaching the point of no return. He hoped the general's plan would be just the medicine needed to take B.J.'s mind off the problem and the bottle. Jake stepped up on the porch and rang the door bell. There was no answer. He rang it again and waited. He could hear someone moving around in the house; then, "Who the hell is it?"

"It's Jake, B.J. Open up."

The door opened slightly and B.J. peeked out at his partner. Mattson had a four-day growth of beard and his eyes were sunken and terribly bloodshot. The man looked like death warmed over. Jake pushed his way past B.J. and walked into the living room. The strong odor of sour milk and stale beer mixed with the heavy aroma of whiskey caused Mortimer's stomach to wrench. God, how could anyone stand to stay in this house more than five minutes without throwing up? Moving to the living room drapes, Jake drew them open then raised the windows. Crossing the room, he did the same to the side windows. Then he went into the kitchen. Ignoring the pile of overflowing garbage that lay scattered on the floor, he opened the window over the sink. Returning to the living room, he found B.J. sitting on the couch, his feet propped on the coffee table, and a bottle of Jack Daniel's in his hand.

"What the fuck, Jake? They make you the new housing inspector or something?"

The fresh air was helping a little, but the smell of whiskey was still overpowering as Jake pushed a pile of empty beer cans out of a chair and sat down facing B.J.

"Damn, B.J.! How in the name of God can you stand it in here?" asked Jake.

"Well, excuse the shit out of me. I didn't realize I was due for an IG inspection this morning," replied B.J. in a slurred voice. "What the fuck you doing here anyway, Navy?"

"First of all, it's three in the afternoon, not morning. Secondly, I just left the general. We're going on a trip tomorrow. We'll be gone three weeks; I thought I should come over and let you know."

Mattson tried to straighten himself up on the couch but found it more work than it was worth. Slumping back into the corner he rested the Jack bottle on the arm of the couch.

"I don't know if I can make this one, Jake. I've been thinking about taking a leave, maybe thirty days or so. I just can't seem to work this out in my mind. It's really getting to me."

"Have you talked to Charlotte lately?"

"Yeah, last night as a matter of fact."

"Well?" asked Jake.

"Well, what? She asked me if I was ready to give it up and find a job out there in the civilian world. If I was, then maybe we had a chance. If I wasn't, then she wished me the best of luck and would appreciate it if I wouldn't call anymore; said it upset the kids too much. Now ain't that a bunch of shit? Damn broad would die before she'd admit it was bothering her as much as it was me. Guess that was always one of our problems—we're just too damn much alike. Neither one wants to admit they might have made a mistake. Oh well, fuck it," said B.J., as he raised the bottle to his lips and took a healthy shot.

Jake shifted slightly in the chair as he watched his partner down the whiskey. He realized this wasn't the best time to try to lecture B.J., but something had to be done.

"Fuck it is exactly what you're doing, B.J. You're fucking up your job, your career, and your life. I've never been in the situation you are right now, but I think if I ever was, I'd find a better way of working it out than drowning myself in a bottle of booze."

Mattson's face twisted up into a look of anger as he leaned forward and stared at Jake through red-lined eyes. "Just who the fuck made you my keeper, asshole? Shit, I was blowin' guys away in 'Nam and drinking a fifth of this stuff every other night while you and those Harvard preppies of yours were still passing out from drinking a six-pack of beer; so don't try and tell me how much I can drink, okay! Who gives a shit, anyway?"

"I do for one. The old man for another, and a hell of a lot of other people in Special Forces and SOCOM that have a rather high level of respect for you and what you've accomplished over the years, that's who. Guys that consider you one of the best in the business, guys that would follow you into hell to pull the devil's tail if that was what you wanted to do. With all that going for you, I would think the least you could do is have a little respect for yourself. Hell, B.J., I know this isn't easy for you, but I think I know you well enough to gamble that you can overcome it. You are not the quitting type, B.J. I believe that. So does the old man. These things have a way of working themselves out. If they don't, then maybe that's just the way it's supposed to be."

Mattson half laughed as he leaned back against the cushions. "Rather like, 'Destiny ordains it so.' Is that it? I would have expected a more philosophical approach from a Harvard man, Jake."

"Sorry to disappoint you, B.J. But like they say, what will be, will be."

B.J. laughed again as he said, "And Jake is saying the major is becoming a drunk. Is that right?"

Jake half grinned as he looked around the room. The fresh air coming through the windows was gradually winning the battle of the odors.

"Well, Major, let's put it this way. Given the condition of your cave here, and you looking like a warmed over turd, I'd say you were fast approaching a rating on the most likely charts."

B.J. was grinning as he slowly turned the Jack bottle on the arm of the couch and said, "Respect, drunk, cave, and warmed over turd. Very nice. So, tell me, oh master of the golden words and silver tongue, just where in hell are we suppose to be taking this charming little three-week vacation this time?"

"Thailand. Full per diem for three weeks."

The bottle stopped in B.J.'s hand as he suddenly sat upright and muttered, "Did you say—Thailand, or am I suffering from an alcohol illusion?"

Jake's smile was wide as he replied, "Three whole weeks' worth at ninety dollars a day, courtesy of Uncle Sam."

Mattson leaned forward and set the bottle of Jack on the coffee table as he said, "I might be feeling a little down, but I'm not nuts. Hell, yes. We'll go to Thailand. Tell me something, Jake. Just what made you and the old man think I was on the edge of becoming an alcoholic?"

Jake leaned forward in his chair, his eyes fixed on a cereal bowl that sat in the middle of the table. Reaching out his hand, he picked up a spoonful of the contents and raised it six inches above the bowl, then let the soggy mixture spill back into the bowl.

"Cocoa Puffs mixed with Jack Daniel's instead of milk

is, I believe, one of the early signs of a possible problem," said Jake, as he dropped the spoon into the bowl. "Think you're ready to drop the self-pity crap and get back to business, B.J.?"

A hurt look came over B.J. as he asked, "Have I been that bad?"

"Pathetic," replied Jake.

"Good thing you never considered becoming a doctor, Jake. Your bedside manner really sucks. You want to help me clean up this mess?"

Jake stood to leave. "No way, partner. You littered the cave, you clean it up. I've got to get home and start packing."

B.J. pulled himself to his feet. He swayed for a moment. Jake reached out and grabbed his arm to steady him as he said, "First thing you need to do is put on some strong coffee, then spend an hour under the shower."

B.J.'s head was starting to beat like a base drum. A familiar sour taste was building up in his mouth, and his stomach was turning flip-flops. He was going to be as sick as a dog in a few minutes. It was only through a strong desire to maintain some small portion of his battered dignity that he was able to prolong the inevitable and walk Jake to the door.

"Are you going to be all right, B.J.?" asked Jake.

Opening the door and squinting his bloodshot eyes against the bright afternoon sunlight, Mattson slapped his partner on the back. "Sure, I'll be fine. Jake—thanks. I really mean that."

The feeling that Jake Mortimer had for Mattson showed clearly in his eyes. It was a caring look, a respectful look. "I'll see you in the morning. General's office. Eight o'clock."

"You got it. Eight on the money," answered B.J.

He stood in the door and waved as Jake backed his car out of the drive and left. Closing the door, he returned to the living room, grabbed up the bottle of Jack and went into the kitchen. Shoving a pile of plates and glasses out of the way, he unscrewed the cap and poured the whiskey down the drain. He knew this did not mean he would never drink again—he enjoyed a drink every now and then—but that was the key: There was a big difference in enjoying a drink and having to have a drink. Without even realizing it, he had placed himself on that thin line that separated the two. It was still possible that he and Charlotte could come to a compromise on the military problem, but an alcohol problem was a totaly different ball game. The bottle emptied, B.J. turned to toss it into the trash. It slipped from his hand and shattered on the floor. He was barefoot. He managed to escape the kitchen without stepping on a piece of the glass. Making it to the living room, he decided it was a good time to take Jake's advice and hit the shower. It was not until he stood in front of the bathroom mirror that he fully understood Jake's remarks about his appearance. He did look like shit. Reaching for his shaving cream, he paused to stare at the trembling left hand, the hand with only four fingers. The index finger had been shot off in a firefight in Vietnam; for a Green Beret Medic who had dreamed of one day becoming a surgeon the dream had ended in the blinking of an eye. A surgeon needed all ten fingers and often wished for more. There were no skilled surgeons with only nine. The finger, the piece of steel in his right leg, and the scars along his side and right shoulder were all marks of his chosen profession: a profession he loved, a profession she hated. Could there ever be a compromise between them? Pressing the top of the can, he formed a small mountain of shaving cream in the palm of the four fingered hand and, leaning toward the mirror, began spreading it over his darkly bearded face as he muttered, "Whatever will be, will be."

CHAPTER 4

The shave, shower, and thirty minutes of puking his guts out had done wonders for B.J. He cleaned the entire house, removed all the old newspapers from the front yard, trashed all the junk mail, and written out checks for the overdue bills. That completed, he went straight to bed and slept a solid ten hours. Another shower at six the next morning, followed by a breakfast of three eggs, bacon, and toast, all downed with a quart of Florida orange juice, had him feeling like a new man. He hadn't felt this good for a long time. Pouring himself a cup of coffee, he went into the living room and flipped the television to the CNN news channel. The Tampa Bay Bucs had lost another close one last night on Monday night football, but their record for the year so far was still respectable.

Relaxing on the couch with his coffee, B.J.'s thoughts drifted to their upcoming trip to Thailand. It was a beautiful country with beautiful and friendly people. He had spent two R & Rs in Bangkok while he was in Vietnam. It was the kind of place that once you were there, you never wanted to leave. A lot of the Special Forces guy hadn't left. When 'Nam ended, they traveled to Thailand, married Thai girls, and started a business, either import/export, nightclubs, or regular bars. Thailand had become their safe haven from the insults, slander, and abuse that greeted the American military men returning from a war that had been lost. B.J.

sometimes wondered why he hadn't stayed with them. Glancing at his watch, he saw it was almost time to leave. He went into the kitchen for one more cup of coffee to take with him. On the news, the reporter was giving details on the arrival in China of Senator Charles Kendell and a group of congressional committee members that were on a good will visit. They would be in China for two days, then travel to India for discussions on economic aid for that country. Accompanying the political dignitaries were their wives and a small staff of personal aides. B.J. picked up the remote as he headed for the door and turned to shut off the television. He hesitated a moment as the camera panned the arriving politicians. A striking young woman with long, brown hair caught B.J.'s attention. She had the prettiest eyes he had ever seen. She was smiling, but there was something about her, something in those eyes that seemed to signal a hidden fear. B.J. moved closer to the television but the camera panned away from her, then the report ended. Switching off the set, B.J. walked out of the house to his car. He could not shake the vision of those haunting eyes as he drove to SOCOM headquarters.

General Raymond Sweet was just stepping out of his car as B.J. pulled into the parking lot. The general made a point of waiting for Major Mattson. Normally, B.J. would have gone out of his way to avoid General Sweet, but this morning he had nothing to fear. For the first time in over a month, there was no alcohol on his breath. His eyes were clear and sparkling. Major B.J. Mattson looked perfectly fit. Saluting smartly as he approached the general, his voice was clear and lively as he said, "Good morning, sir. Beautiful day, isn't it?"

Sweet's squinty eyes registered the disappointment he felt at seeing Mattson in such fine shape. He had been led to believe that the man was on the verge of an alcoholic breakdown. Stepping a little closer to the major as he returned the salute, his rodent nose wrinkled slightly as he sniffed for the telltale odor of alcohol. There was none, but

Sweet's obvious dislike for Mattson would not allow him to let the man slip by without some sort of belittling.

"Well, I see you have found an opportunity in your very busy schedule to honor us with a few hours' work, Major, I'm sure the taxpayers will be as appreciative as I am. Tell me, Major, how are your marital problems working out?" The question was followed by an overzealous smile. Sweet was loving this.

B.J. considered telling the short, fat man to go to hell; it wasn't any of his business. A few days ago that is exactly what he would have done—and possibly even decked the little bastard in the bargain. But for now, he felt too good to let the Pentagon's number one prick ruin his day.

"Sir, if you will check with General Johnson, you will find that I have been on comp time for the last two weeks. As far as my family is concerned, my wife and the kids are spending the summer with her parents at their ranch in Oklahoma and having a wonderful time, from what I understand. Now, if you'll excuse me, sir. I have a meeting to attend." Mattson clicked his heels together loudly and saluted once more, then pivoted smartly on his heel and walked away.

Sweet's stomach burned like fire as he watched the tall Texan go through the double glass doors of the headquarters. Sweet had an ulcer that bothered him on occasion, but never as badly as when he was around Mattson and that wisecracking Navy SEAL, Mortimer. He was still going to get them both. It might take longer than he had planned, but sooner or later they were going to screw up, and when they did, he would be right there. He owed them for the Ecuador business. They had made him look like a fool, not only to the chiefs of staff, but in the eyes of the president himself. Only behind-the-scenes action by friends from the National Security Agency had saved him from becoming a laughingstock on the nightly news. He was not about to forget that.

The ideal situation would be to get not only Mattson and Mortimer, but General Johnson as well. Without him in command of SOCOM it would be a simple matter to have this bunch of self-styled Rambos deactivated and reassigned to the regular army where they would be forced to learn discipline or be thrown out of the service. He would receive a promotion and another star while the joint chiefs would see the appropriations money that had been cut from their budgets to support these supposed high tech warriors returned to their coffers. "Yes," smiled Sweet as he headed for the two story building. "It is just a matter of time." In the end, he would get them all: Mattson, Mortimer, Johnson, and SOCOM. No one made a fool of Raymond Sweet.

Jake was standing by the information desk talking with Master Sergeant Tommy Smith, Senior Crew Chief of the Special Aviation Wing assigned to Special Operations Command. If it hadn't been for the timely arrival of Smith and two helicopter gunships in Ecuador, Jake Mortimer would now be history. Smith knew his way around just about every kind of aircraft that could get off the ground. He was a twenty year man with vast experience and a deep love for the special operations concept.

"How's it going this morning, Major?" asked Smith as he reached out his hand and clasped B.J.'s tightly in his own. He was glad to see the major looking so well. The Smiths and the Mattsons had been close friends. Charlotte had left a letter with Nancy Smith when she left. Giving that letter to B.J. at the Tampa airport had been one of the hardest things Nancy Smith had ever had to do. B.J. smiled at the stockily built crew chief and nodded to Jake as he replied, "Doing just fine, Tommy. How's the wife and kids?"

"Couldn't be better, B.J. I was just telling Jake, I got a report on that young captain who was wounded in that shoot-out you had at the governors place down south."

"Oh yeah. Kid's name was Jackson—Mark Jackson. How's he doing?"

"Came out smelling like a rose. He'll be out of the hospital and on convalescent leave by the end of the week. Just thought you'd like to know."

"Thanks, Tommy." Turning to Jake, B.J. winked as he

said, "Guess we've got a pretty busy schedule ahead of us today, don't we Commander?"

Mortimer grinned as he slapped B.J. on the back. There was look of pride in his eyes. Now this was the B.J. Mattson he knew and respected.

"You got it, boss. The general is waiting for us in his office."

The three parted company, with B.J. and Jake promising to keep a dinner date at the Smith home when they returned from their trip.

General Johnson's aide saw the two officers approaching and waved for them to go right in. Ol' Q-Tip glanced up from some paperwork he was signing and motioned for the visitors to take a seat. While they waited for him to finish, B.J. noticed the picture sitting at one corner of the desk. It was Johnson and his son standing by a Blackhawk helicopter. The picture had been taken only days before young Captain Johnson had been shot down and killed during the Grenada invasion. The ironic part was that he hadn't been shot down by Cubans, but by U.S. forces. This was only one of the tragedies of that massive military fiasco that had been hidden from the public. There were plenty more, but B.J. doubted very seriously if they would ever be revealed—in his lifetime, anyway.

Laying his pen aside, Johnson leaned back in his chair and stared at the two men he had unofficially designated as his personal troubleshooters and most trusted advisors. He was especially pleased to see that B.J. looked every bit the clean-cut, hard charging officer he knew he was. This little jaunt to Thailand was going to be just the thing for him.

"Gentlemen, your orders are ready and waiting at the finance office. You will be paid in advance per diem this morning and you will be on your way to Fort Lewis, Washington by this afternoon. Tomorrow morning you will be briefed on the details of the training exercise. By tomorrow afternoon, you should be on your way to Bangkok. I expect you both to make maximum use of this three week exercise. Remember you are there to observe and offer suggestions when necessary. You must make sure that at no time do you undermine the authority or the leadership of the SOCOM commanders involved in this exercise. As I have stated, you are there only to evaluate their proficiency. Is that understood?"

Jake and B.J. both nodded that they fully understood their responsibilities.

"Very good, then," said Johnson. "That will be all, gentlemen. Have a good trip. I'll see you in three weeks."

Mattson and Mortimer stood and saluted, then headed for the door. B.J. was about to follow Jake out of the office when Johnson said, "B.J.!"

Mattson turned and, standing at attention, replied, "Yes, sir."

Johnson had a fatherly smile on his face as he softly said, "Good to have you back with us, son."

After the two months of the personal hell and torment that B.J. had been going through, that smile and those words meant more than the general realized.

"Thank you, sir. Thank you for everything." Saluting again, Major B. J. Mattson spun smartly on his heel and left the office. He felt ten feet tall as he strolled down the hall to catch up with Jake. He had just gained two things in his life that had been sorely missing lately: confidence and pride. It showed. He even smiled at General Sweet as they passed him in the hall—a gesture that seemed to cause the two star general sudden and extensive pain in the stomach area.

Mattson placed his suitcases by the front door. Jake would be by to pick him up in a few minutes for the drive to the airport. Making a final check of the house to be sure that everything was turned off, he switched on the small table lamp by the couch so that the house would not be totally dark at night. As he was stepping back from the light, his eyes fixed on the phone. He stared at it for a long moment, then picked it up and dialed the familiar long distance number. As the phone began to ring on the other end, he considered hanging up, but it was too late.

"Hello," came the soft voice he had heard next to him in

bed for so many years. Even that simple word sent a flood of mixed emotions flowing through him. His mouth had suddenly gone dry. This had been a bad idea.

"Hi— Hi, Charlotte."

There was a pause of a few seconds that seemed like hours before she answered.

"Hello, B.J. How are you?"

"Fine—I'm doing fine. How about you and the kids?"

He could sense the same pain and longing in her gentle voice.

"We're fine. The kids really do miss you, B.J. They know things are wrong, and they try to understand, but it's hard for them. They wouldn't ask, but they want to know when this will be over and we can be a family again. I don't know what I could tell them if they did ask." She paused a moment, then asked, "Have you thought about us, B.J.?"

"More than you know, Charlotte."

"B.J., take a few weeks' leave and come out here. It's so peaceful and quiet. We could go for walks like we used to. We can talk this thing out; I know we can. Please, just for a little while."

"I—I can't, Charlotte. Jake and I are leaving this afternoon."

The deep sigh that came over the phone spread a blanket of guilt over him. Here she was trying to work this out, and as usual he was leaving and there was no time. That had been her point all along. There was never time enough for them.

"Charlotte—I—I have to tell you, I—" A loud blast from a car horn in the driveway interrupted him. It was Jake.

"That's all right, B.J. Don't worry about it."

"But I do worry, Charlotte. I worry that if we don't fix this soon, it will be too late. We—" The horn blared again, only longer this time.

"Is that Jake, honking for you?" she asked.

"Yes."

"You had better go then. B.J., be—be careful. We love you. Bye."

She hung up before he could answer. Staring at the silent receiver in his hand, he whispered, "I love you, too."

The sight of the Great Wall of China had taken Kathryn Nickleson's breath away. She could remember seeing pictures of the historic wall while a student in high school and college, but no picture could possibly capture the true size and presence of the wall itself. Edward Nickleson and Mrs. Kendell had comforted her throughout the long flight, reassuring her that the more she traveled by air, the easier it would become. Their reassurance had proven to be correct. Their three day visit to China now completed, Kathryn once again found herself in an airport waiting to board an airplane for New Delhi, India, and the second leg of their Southeast Asian tour. Surprisingly, she found the sight of the approaching aircraft caused only a slight flutter in her stomach, which quickly disappeared as Edward slipped his strong arm around her waist and said, "How are we doing, darling?"

Placing her small hand over his, she smiled and whispered, "Just fine, Mr. Congressman. You were right. This trip is fabulous. I'm so glad you insisted that I come along." Patting the arm wrapped around her waist, she stretched on her tiptoes and gave him a kiss on the cheek.

"Here, here, now. We can't have any of that decadent Western world type of smut like open kissing going on in front of the Chinese. You two newlyweds will just have to wait until we're on the plane."

Kathryn blushed as she turned and smiled at Diane Meeker, the wife of Congressman Howard Meeker, from Florida. Of the three other congressional wives accompanying their husbands on this trip, Diane was the one that Kathryn felt the closest to. They were both the same age and Diane's wit and charm had proven to be a comfort on the long trip. Her husband Howard had already served one term and been elected to a second. Kathryn was pleased to find someone who could fully understand her nervousness and desire to always do or say the right thing. Diane had given her all the do's and don'ts expected of an elected official's wife. She had especially emphasized the don'ts, relating all the mistakes that she had made during that first term. They had become very close friends in a short time.

"Edward, I think I have embarrassed your lovely wife. I haven't seen that bright a red on a fire engine," laughed Diane.

"Oh, Diane, listen to you. I just forget sometimes that China hasn't gone totally Western yet. Who knows? I may have sparked a whole new revolution by showing open affection in China."

"You might at that," grinned Diane. "Edward, would you mind if I steal this revolutionary away from you for a few minutes? We'd like to get a group shot of just the wives together in front of the airport."

"By all means. See you in a little while, darling," replied Nickleson, as he gave her a peck on the cheek, then looked around slyly as if to see if anyone was watching. The girls were still laughing as he watched them go out the front doors. It was good to see her laughing, thought Edward as he sat down on one of the long, hard benches and lit a cigarette. Across the way, standing near the ticket counter, he saw Senator Kendell and the two personal bodyguards talking with what appeared to be a Chinese general. The two large, brown suitcases that had been loaded in Washington sat next to the group. Nickleson was still puzzled by the attention the suitcases received. On their arrival in China, they had been the first bags unloaded under the personal supervision of the senator himself with the ever present bodyguards waiting to take charge of them. It could mean nothing, but Edward Nickleson found it strange.

"Mind if I join you, Edward?"

Nickleson looked up to see Congressman Howell of New York pulling a pack of cigarettes from his shirt pocket.

"No, not at all. Please, do."

Howell lit his smoke then plopped his overweight frame down next to Nickleson on the bench.

"Jesus, you'd think with all the advances these people are making, they could afford to put some decent damn seating in their airport. This wooden thing is hard on the butt."

Nickleson had only heard part of what Howell was saying. His attention was drawn to the group around the bags. The general had pointed to the brown leather and then at Kendell. It appeared as if there was an argument. The senator was looking around nervously and trying to get the general to lower his voice. Mr. Alfonso and Mr. Rivera had quickly moved to the senator's side and placed their hands in their coats at about the level where their shoulder holsters would be. If Nickleson didn't know any better, he would swear they were about to have a shoot-out right here in the airport. The general motioned with his hand and five Chinese soldiers suddenly appeared at his side. It was clear that Kendell was trying to calm the situation. He said something to the two bodyguards and they removed their hands from their jackets. He then pointed to a side door beyond the security barrier, and the general nodded his approval. The bags were picked up and the entire group, soldiers and all, disappeared through the door. Within seconds, two more soldiers came from behind the ticket counter and took up positions on each side of the door.

"Don't you think so, Edward?" asked Howell.

"Wha—what? Oh, I'm sorry Thomas, I was distracted for a moment. What were you saying?"

"The seats, Edward, these sixteenth-century pieces of petrified wood that they expect a person to sit on. They could surely do better than this, don't you think so?"

Nickleson still had his eyes fixed on the door as he answered, "Yes. Of course. Thomas, let me ask you something. You've been on the Hill for over ten years. Have you gone on many of these trips with the senator?"

"Oh yes. I take Martha on two or three a year. Beats the hell out of paying a travel agent a fortune."

"How many have you been on with Senator Kendell?"

Thomas Howell seemed a little puzzled by the question.

"I'm not sure, Edward. Eight, maybe nine. Why?"

"Does he always take his own personal bodyguards with him?"

"No. Now that you mention it, I believe I've only seen them come along when we travel to Southeast Asia. Why?

Just what are you getting at, Edward? You're beginning to sound more like the CIA than an elected official. Why the sudden interest in Kendell's security?"

Thomas Howell had a good point. It wasn't any of his business why the senator only took security with him when he traveled in Asia. What was wrong with that? Besides, what did a freshman congressman from Iowa know about anything? God! He was getting as paranoid about those suitcases as Kathryn was about flying.

"So, what is it, Edward? Why the twenty questions?" asked Howell.

"It's nothing, Thomas. I was just curious, that's all."

Before Howell could ask any more questions, the PA system emitted a sharp screeching sound followed by a pleasant woman's voice announcing that the flight for New Delhi was now loading at gate number two and would ticket holders please report for ticket verification.

"Well, that's us, Edward. We'd better see if we can round up the ladies," said Howell as he gave out a loud groan and pushed his chubby body up from the hard seat. "God, my hemorrhoids would have hemorrhoids if I sat on these damn things any longer."

Nickleson rose to his feet and watched as the senator and the small group came out of the side room. Kendell's face appeared flushed, and the look on the faces of the two bodyguards was anything but pleasant. The only smiling face in the group belonged to the Chinese general. His grin was so wide that Nickleson could see the man's pearly white teeth from across the room. The general reached out to shake hands with Kendell, who hesitated for a moment, then briefly touched the man's hand, quickly pulling it back and turning to walk away. The bodyguards followed with the bags.

Nickleson purposely waited until Kendell was near the bench, then he fell in beside him, matching him stride for stride.

"Is there a problem, Senator?" he asked.

Kendell snapped his head in Nickleson's direction. Without breaking stride, he answered in a clearly hostile voice.

"Congressman, you let me take care of the problems on this trip, okay? You're just along for the ride, so let's keep it that way, all right?"

Nickleson was shocked at the senator's harsh tone and wild-eyed look. Whatever had occurred in that room had Kendell on the verge of uncontrollable rage. Nodding in compliance to the senator's words, Nickleson slowed his pace and let Kendell continue by himself. The bodyguards brushed past him, the one called Rivera giving him a threatening look as he quickened his step to catch up with Kendell. Nickleson didn't know what was going on, but whatever it was, Kendell had no intention of sharing it with the rest of the group. That was obvious as Nickleson watched the three other senators traveling with them receive the same treatment when they attempted to ask questions. Kendell waved them off as he hastened to the loading area. The three senators turned to Nickleson as he approached.

"Jesus, Ed, what the hell's wrong with Charlie?" asked Senator Hayden of Kansas.

"You got me, Senator. But whatever it is, it sure has him upset."

The last call for their flight came over the PA system. They all agreed on one thing. If the senator wanted to talk, they were willing to listen. Otherwise, no one had any intention of incurring the further wrath of Charles Kendell, particularly not a freshman congressman. Still, Nickleson couldn't help but be concerned about what was going on: the obsession with the suitcases; the two bodyguards that looked more like extras from the movie *The Godfather* than actual security personnel; and the encounter with a Chinese general and his troops that had teetered on the verge of guns being drawn. He may be just a virgin congressman, but he wasn't blind. Something was very wrong, and he had Kathryn to think of. Senator Kendell might not like it, but he was going to have to answer some questions, and answer them soon. Nickleson would let it go for now, but once they were in New Delhi, he was going to find out just what was so special about those suitcases.

CHAPTER 5

Don Muang International Airport, located just outside Bangkok, was busy as usual. Buddhist monks, wrapped in their traditional saffron robes, made their way around crowds of businessmen in lightweight Hagger suits and leather briefcases. Thai women with long, flowing black hair and light-brown complexions moved gracefully about in their colorful Panung pants, while others had adopted the modern Western look. No matter what they wore, they were still among the most beautiful women in the world.

Mattson and Mortimer picked their way through the flurry of activity and headed for the luggage area. For B. J. Mattson, it was like returning to an old hometown. The airport was larger and more modern than he remembered, but the warm, damp, flower-laden smell and the feel of Southeast Asia was still the same. The ever smiling faces of the Thai people and the kaleidoscope of old memories that flashed through his mind gave him a feeling of inner peace that he had not known for some time. He was glad he was here.

"Major Mattson, Commander Mortimer." Both officers stopped at hearing their names and turned to face a tall lieutenant colonel who had disengaged himself from the continuous flood of people that flowed steadily back and forth along the main corridor. The colonel was dressed in camouflage fatigues. There was a distinctive black beret, with the flash and crest of the 75th Rangers, cocked smartly above his left eye. Mattson guessed the man to be in his early forties and judging from the wide chest and well-developed arms emerging from the neatly rolled sleeves of the fatigue shirt, the colonel was in excellent condition. Standing next to him was an older man with graying hair and thick glasses that made his brown eyes seem overly large. He was in his late fifties and wore a light blue walking suit that had obviously been tailor-made to hide a drooping stomach that had seen more than its share of beer. Extending a chubby hand to Mattson, he smiled, displaying tobacco stained teeth, and spoke in a high-pitched voice.

"Major Mattson, I'm Marshall Parsons, Deputy Chief of Mission here in Thailand. This is Lieutenant Colonel Mark Decker, commander of the 2nd Ranger Battalion."

Mattson shook hands with both men as he said, "Pleasure to meet you, gentlemen." Turning to Jake he continued, "This is Lieutenant Commander Jacob Mortimer." Jake nodded to both men as he shook their hands.

"Major, if you and the commander will let me have your claim checks, I will see that your luggage is picked up and delivered to the Ambassador Hotel. We took the liberty of securing two rooms for you. It is only a short distance from the embassy and I'm sure you will find the accommodations quite suitable."

"Thank you, Mr. Parsons," replied B.J. as he handed the man their claim checks. Glancing over at the colonel, he continued, "I assume it is a company from your battalion that we will be evaluating, Colonel Decker."

Decker's gravelly voice seemed to fit his six-foot-four frame. "Yes, Major Mattson, Bravo Company, 2nd Battalion of the 75th Rangers, already at the training site at Chiang Mai and presently conducting refresher classes on tactics and weapons. The actual training exercise will begin in three days. I have a detailed briefing scheduled for two this afternoon at the embassy. I'm sure that any questions you may have will be answered at that briefing, Major."

"Yes, yes. We have everything taken care of, Major. Now if you'll come along, I'll have my driver drop you at the hotel so you can freshen up and get a little rest before this afternoon," said Parsons as he pulled a pocket watch from his vest and checked the time.

Mortimer smiled as he watched Parsons turn on his heel and take hurried little steps, to ease his short, chubby, five-foot-three body into the mainstream of human traffic swarming through the airport. B.J. saw the smile and asked what was so funny.

"Just watching that little man there reminded me of that rabbit in *Alice in Wonderland*. You know, always checking his watch and in a hurry."

Decker laughed as he said, "Better get used to it, fellows. Parsons is a real stickler for punctuality. But don't be fooled by the pop bottle glasses and the beer belly. The guy has his shit together and can pull a hell of a lot of strings to get you whatever you need, any time you need it. Just don't be late picking it up."

"Thanks, Colonel. Sounds like a good man to know. Well, Mr. Mortimer, shall we be off to the hotel and a spot of tea?" asked B.J.

Jake Mortimer was still smiling, but this time it was because of B.J. It was hard to believe that this was the same man who only a week ago had been drowning himself in self-pity and a bottle. Being in Asia less than ten minutes had already made a new man of B.J. Mattson. His eyes were clear, and he appeared excited and ready to get to work for the first time in weeks. Best of all, he had regained that special Mattson sense of humor. "Absolutely splendid idea, Mr. Mattson. After you," answered Jake as he bent slightly at the waist and swung his hand out in the direction of the shifting crowds.

Colonel Decker fell in behind the two officers as they made their way into the crowd and were caught up in the human tide sweeping toward the front doors of the airport. Outside, Marshall Parsons stood impatiently glancing at his timepiece and watching the elderly red cap, who had secured their bags, slowly place one bag at a time in the trunk of the embassy staff car. Seeing the three officers exit the main building he tapped his fingers on the top of the car and shouted, "Hurry now, gentlemen, we are three minutes behind schedule."

The three men grinned at each other as Mortimer whispered, "I'm late. I'm late. I'm late for a very important date. I'm late, I'm late, I'm late."

Colonel Decker bade the two officers good-bye at the hotel. He would see them at 1400 hours for the briefing. Parsons stayed only long enough to make sure that there were no problems with their accommodations; then he, too, departed. The hotel had a pleasant atmosphere. The scent of stir-fried Oriental vegetables and sizzling steak came from the direction of the main dining room. The faint sound of rock music came from beyond the closed doors of the Bamboo Lounge.

The temptation to head straight for the bar and a drink after the long trip weighed heavily on Mattson's mind. Jake could see the look on B.J.'s face. He wouldn't mind having a drink himself.

B.J. pondered the idea for a moment, then decided against it. Maybe later tonight, after supper. Right now he was just tired, and the thought of a short nap before the briefing sounded more inviting. He noticed Jake tapping his foot to the faint sound of the music from inside.

"Jake, if you want to get a drink, go ahead. I think I'll get a little sack time before we head over to the embassy."

"You're sure you won't mind, B.J.?"

"Hell, what's to mind? It ain't like we're sleeping together, you know."

Jake gave him the dimpled grin, "You got it, man. See you later."

B.J. got his key from the desk clerk and went to his room. After a long, hot shower and a shave, B. J. Mattson was fast asleep within minutes after his head hit the pillow.

Fortunately, Mattson had left a message with the front desk to give him a call at 1330 hours. The phone awakened him from a sound sleep. The rigors of the long flight and jet lag had taken its toll. Realizing they only had thirty minutes to get to the embassy, he threw on his clothes, hurried across the hall, and began beating on Jake's door. Mortimer opened it slightly. He had a towel wrapped around his waist, and judging from his eyes, he had been asleep.

"Let's move it, Jake. We've got twenty minutes to be at the embassy."

"Uh—yeah—okay. Twenty minutes, you say?"

"Yeah. Unless you want to catch hell from the White Rabbit for being late. You better move it." B.J. paused a moment, then said, "Jesus, Jake. I thought I was tired. You look like shit. Didn't you get any rest?"

Before Jake could answer, Mattson caught a glimpse of the perfectly shaped bare ass of a tall, long-legged Thai girl as she made a dash for the bathroom. Her waist-length, coal black hair swinging wildly as she spun to close the door.

Jake managed a weak smile, as he said, "Must be jet lag."

"My ass!" laughed B.J. "More like pussy lag! See you downstairs. Five minutes."

"You got it."

B.J. was still laughing as he turned and headed for the elevator. "No, partner, I believe you're the one that got it."

Mattson and Mortimer entered the briefing room with exactly two minutes to spare. True to form, Marshall Parsons was standing by the door with his gold pocket watch in hand as they walked through the doors.

The briefing presented by Lieutenant Colonel Decker and his very efficient staff lasted less than thirty minutes. It was the standard training operation, broken down into three one-week phases. In the first week, the 75th Rangers would provide the Thai Special Forces with the latest innovations in classroom and field teaching techniques as well as demonstrations of the new models of small arms and their effectiveness in counterinsurgency operations. During the second week, the teachers would become the pupils and the Thais would become the instructors. The Rangers would be shown the latest methods of tracking and jungle camouflage, as well as trail interdiction and river crossings. The final week would be a joint operation against an aggressor force made up of members of the Royal Thai Third Army, responsible for all military actions in the northern regions. The SOCOM training concept would prove highly valuable to the members of both countries, and it sure beat the old system of boring classrooms and slide shows. Training exercises exactly like this one were going on in all parts of the world. On any given day, there were no less than ten SOCOM teams, teaching as well as being taught, scattered around the globe. It was a concept that had been developed by the SOCOM boss, General Jonathan J. Johnson, who believed that the only way a soldier can learn is by putting him on the ground and letting him do it. The troops loved it. The brass in Washington hated it. The training wasn't cheap, and the money came from the budget of each branch of the military services.

Lieutenant Colonel Decker concluded the briefing by giving Jake and B.J. the times for movement from the hotel to the airport and the flight time from Bangkok to Chiang Mai Airport. There they would be met by the company commander and his executive officer for the trip to the training camp where they would be introduced to the various teams conducting the different phases of training. Colonel Decker would not be going at this time but would join them in a few days.

The briefing completed, Mattson and Mortimer remained at the embassy for another hour for coffee and small talk, then excused themselves and returned to the hotel. They made a quick trip to the Bamboo Lounge for a few drinks, with B.J. limiting himself to two. Jake wanted to go out and see the town. B.J. begged off: He was still worn out. The month of heavy drinking and limited exercise had taken its toll. Once the training mission was over, they would go out together before the flight home. Jake had started to argue the point with his partner but could tell B.J. had made up his mind; he wasn't going.

"Okay, B.J. I'll see you later," said Jake as he walked to the front door.

B.J. was waiting for the elevator and feeling that he had

somehow let Jake down by not going out on the town with him. Twenty years ago no one could have kept him in this hotel for two minutes, but that was twenty years before, and before Charlotte. No matter how hard he tried to concentrate on the business at hand, he couldn't get her out of his mind. She was so much a part of his life and he missed her. It was not the kind of feeling he wanted to have while touring the bars of Bangkok. But damn, he hated to leave Jake by himself.

That problem suddenly vanished as the long-legged girl who had been in Jake's room earlier came down the stairs in one of the shortest leather miniskirts B.J. had ever seen. The girl had legs that went all the way to her ass. And what a body. She called out to Jake just as he was about to go out the door, then ran up to him; her ample breasts bounced beneath a sheer white blouse that left little to the imagination. It was a good thing that Jake was a Navy SEAL and in great condition. He was going to need every bit of his strength to get out of bed in the morning. The bell on the elevator rang and the door opened. As B.J. stepped inside, he watched his partner go out the front door with his arm around the Thai girl's waist, her perfectly round ass straining against the leather skirt.

"I must be getting old," whispered B.J. to himself as he punched the button on the elevator. "Two shots of Jack Daniel's and a piece of that would kill me!" The door slid shut, and the old man went to his room to get some sleep.

Edward Nickleson finished his tea and left the hotel restaurant. He had tried on two occasions to get Senator Kendell alone that morning before the meeting with India's prime minister and the representatives of his parliament, but the senator had insisted he was far too busy. Perhaps in the afternoon they could get together. Well, it was afternoon and the wives had gone on a trip to the city of Agra to visit the famed Taj Mahal. This would be a perfect time to try to get some answers to a few questions. He had invited Thomas Howell to come along with him, but the congressman from New York had declined: Kendell was still in a foul mood, and it was best to leave him alone until he was in better spirits. He was the kind of man one could ill afford to have as an enemy, especially if you expected to stay in Washington any length of time. Nickleson had sat quietly drinking his tea and considering Howell's advice. Kendell was a powerful man, that was true enough, but the incident at the China airport still bothered him. He wanted some answers.

Stepping from the elevator on Kendell's floor, Nickleson found the room and knocked on the door.

Rivera answered the door, a look of contempt on his face. "What do you want?" he growled in broken English.

"I need to see Senator Kendell. Tell him its Congressman Nickleson."

"I know who you are, gringo," replied Rivera in a sarcastic tone. "The senator, he is sleeping, he no want to be bothered. Maybe you come back later."

The man was lying. Nickleson could hear Kendell's voice coming from the back bedroom. He was obviously talking to someone on the phone. Nickleson overheard him yelling, "Hello—hello—yeah, I said the bastard charged us double this time. Yeah that's right—fucking double, do you hear me?" There was a pause, then another outburst, "Well screw you! Maybe you should be handling this deal then."

Nickleson tried to peer around the bodyguard and nodded toward the room as he said, "It would seem that the senator is awake now. I'll just—" The congressman had pushed against the door to enter the room but found Rivera's foot planted firmly against it. He pushed Nickleson back with one hand while reaching into his coat where the shoulder holster hung, with the other.

"You are mistaken, señor. You leave now, come back later." With that, Rivera shoved Nickleson back even farther and slammed the door in his face. Nickleson was pissed now. Stepping back to the door, he beat on it like a man obsessed. Bodyguard or no bodyguard, Rivera couldn't treat a congressman that way.

The door suddenly swung open and Nickleson found himself staring up at the six-foot-six gorilla of a man that

Kendell had called Mr. Alfonso. The strong odor of whiskey caused Nickleson to take a step back as the huge man squared his broad shoulders in the doorway and pointed his finger in the congressman's face. "Now look, buddy, my friend done told you to come back later. The senator's got no time for chitchat, so move it on outta here."

The man's size alone was enough to intimidate Nickleson. He was going to see Kendell, but not this afternoon. Without saying another word, Alfonso shut the door. Nickleson cursed under his breath as he turned and walked back to the elevator. He was surer now than ever that something was going on, and Kendell was involved up to his ass in whatever it was. He had come up here to get some answers, and now he found himself leaving with even more questions. Who was Kendell talking to? Who did he have to pay double? And for what? Who did those creeps Rivera and Alfonso really work for? Stepping into the elevator, he considered punching the button that would take him to Congressman Howell's floor. Maybe if they sifted among the multitude of questions together, they could possibly come up with some answers that made sense. The thought was just that, a thought. Howell, as well as the other members of the Washington elite on this trip, had already expressed no great desire to tangle with a man like Kendell. Frustrated, Nickleson pressed the button for his floor. If he was going to have to figure this out by himself, then so be it. They were leaving for Bangkok in the morning. It was going to be interesting to see how Kendell was going to avoid him on the plane. He only wanted two things from the Senator: first, some answers and second, an apology from those two goons, Alfonso and Rivera.

Stepping from the Lear Jet into the bright morning sunlight, Mattson glanced at his watch. Parsons's demand for punctuality seemed to have carried over to the embassy drivers and pilots as well. Their arrival at the Chiang Mai Airport was right on schedule. Beyond the security fence of the VIP arrival area three men dressed in jungle fatigues and black berets stood in front of three jeeps. Behind the wheel of each vehicle sat a Thai Special Forces soldier in jungles and a red beret. Seeing Mattson exit the aircraft, the three Americans made their way through the gate and toward the plane. Jake shaded his eyes and stared at the men as they approached.

"Looks like the welcoming committee is here," he said.

"Yeah," replied B.J. "You know, I'm beginning to think that our boy Parsons has this whole country running on time."

All three of the Rangers were big men, averaging from six feet to six-foot-three and weighing in at anywhere from 200 to 220 pounds. They stood tall and straight as they made their way to the plane. The silver bars on the beret of the first man glistened in the sunlight as he halted a few feet in front of B.J. The other two men stood at rigid attention just behind the captain, who now brought his hand up smartly and saluted.

"Sir, Captain Edward Ross, Commander, B Company, 75th Rangers."

Both B.J. and Jake returned the salute, then shook hands with the captain who then introduced his executive officer, Lieutenant Bill Jacoby and Sergeant Major Dan McKinney. More handshakes were exchanged all around, and the group headed for the jeeps while two Thai soldiers secured the luggage, consisting of two bulging aviator kit bags and one regular suitcase.

"How's everything down in SOCOM land, Major?" asked the blue-eyed captain with the closely cropped blond hair as the jeep pulled out onto the main highway.

"Just fine, Captain Ross. How about the training? Any problems?" asked B.J.

"No, sir. We have a pretty sharp bunch of troops, Major. They're loving every minute of this trip. They are really getting involved with their Thai counterparts and putting out 110 percent. We couldn't ask for more from them."

"Sounds good, Captain. Mighty good," replied Mattson as he leaned back in the seat of the jeep, planted his foot comfortably against the glove compartment, and took in the beauty of the Thai countryside.

Jake was riding in the second jeep with Lieutenant Jacoby and Sergeant Major McKinney. The lieutenant leaned forward, raising his voice in order to be heard above the wind whipping around the uncovered jeep, and said, "Commander Mortimer, sir, just wanted to let you know that the boys of Company B are honored to have you and the major as our evaluators on this exercise. We read about the job you both did down in Ecuador. You're kind of like heroes to a lot of the guys out here. It's going to be a real pleasure working with you."

Jake half turned in the seat and gave the lieutenant a thumbs-up. The sergeant major simply shrugged his shoulders as if to say, "Hey, what'd you want me say?" Heroes, thought Jake as he turned back around and rested his jungle boot on the side panel of the jeep. They hadn't seen the sweat running down his face from fear, nor his trembling hands as the Ecuadorian commandos has charged their position that day. There had been little thought of heroics then, only the thought of staying alive. Jake didn't care much for the idea of being held up as some kind of hero. It was a title he did not want, a title that somehow didn't seem right when applied to that day when so many people had been killed. He could still hear the screams of the wounded and the dying as if it had only happened minutes ago. He may be a lot of things, but a hero wasn't one of them.

The trip from the airport had taken thirty minutes. As the jeeps swung onto the dusty road that led to the training camp, Mattson saw the first triple rows of concertina barbed wire and the machine gun towers that flanked each side of the entrance to the compound. Beyond the gates, two rows of men in both black and red berets were lined along each side of the road as an honor guard. As the jeep neared the gate, he heard one of the soldiers yell, "Present arms," and the two rows neatly snapped their weapons to the proper position. Mattson and Mortimer saluted the honor guard as they passed.

"All this fuss wasn't really necessary, Captain," said B.J. as they pulled up in front of the camp headquarters.

Hopping from the jeep, Ross smiled as he said, "Wasn't

my idea, Major. The boys did that one on their own. Hope you didn't mind."

"Hell, what's there to mind? Us old Texas boys don't get that kind of treatment every day."

A Thai colonel in a form-fitting set of jungle fatigues came down the bamboo steps of the headshed and stopped a few feet short of Mattson.

"Major Mattson, Commander Mortimer, I'd like you to meet Colonel Chao Fa Chakkri. Colonel Chakkri is the commander of the Special Forces troops in the Third Army district as well as the border forces to the north."

B.J. and Jake saluted, waiting until the colonel had dropped his hand before they reached out and shook hands with the Thai leader. Chakkri's grip was firm and friendly. His smile was warm and genuine as he said, "We are happy to have you both here, Major, Commander. Hopefully our humble learnings shall meet with your satisfaction. Captain Ross's men have provided us with excellent instruction since their arrival. I assure you, such talent has not been wasted. My soldiers are always eager to learn."

Jake and B.J. had read the file on Colonel Chakkri during the briefing presented by Lieutenant Colonel Decker. The man was a hard charger and a firm believer in the use of unconventional warfare to eliminate Communist insurgents and secure the borders of Thailand. Chakkri had attended the National Defense College, one of the highest-level military schools in the country, as well as The Armed Forces Staff College, both in Thailand. His schooling in the United States had included the Airborne and Ranger schools at Fort Benning, Georgia, the Special Forces Officer Course at Fort Bragg, North Carolina, and the Staff College at Fort Leavenworth, Kansas. His courage as well as his knowledge of tactics had been tested countless times along the Laotian and Burmese borders, where he, with his Special Forces troops and border guards, faced almost daily firefights with Communist insurgents, bandits, drug lords and renegades. The colonel had been wounded four times over the past three years. He was not a commander who conducted operations from behind a desk or from the safety of a heavily armed headquarters, a fact that had endeared him to the troops of his command.

"Just as I am sure our rangers will learn much from your soldiers, Colonel," said Jake.

Chakkri nodded his approval at the statement and smiled as he said, "Gentlemen, if you will follow Major Rama, my adjutant, he will show you to your quarters. We have planned a special dinner for tonight in your honor. It shall begin at seven. Until then, I am certain you will want to visit with Captain Ross and his Rangers. Until tonight, then, gentlemen." Chakkri saluted smartly. The American contingent snapped to attention and returned the salute, holding theirs until Chakkri had departed.

"I'd say that man has a firm grip on his position around here, Captain," said B.J. as they followed Major Rama across the compound to their quarters.

"You got that right, sir," replied Ross. "He's a natural born leader and this Third Army of his would follow him anywhere. That's something that hasn't gone unnoticed by more than a few generals back at supreme headquarters. Chakkri makes them nervous. He knows that, and he loves it. You see, he's a personal friend of the king's son. He and the prince were at the Special Warfare School at Fort Bragg together. Chakkri wants to make sure that any of those generals in Bangkok that might be playing with the idea of a military takeover here in Thailand know they're going to have to deal with him and his Third Army. From what I gather, that very fact has ended a lot of back room plotting the last few years. The king is lucky to have a man like Chakkri around."

"Seems strange that an officer that loyal and with all his experience would only hold the rank of colonel," said Jake.

Ross frowned as he answered, "Yeah. No shit. That's just the way it is around these parts, Commander."

"Let me guess," said B.J. "Colonel Chakkri's a hell of a soldier and a close friend of the royal family, but he was born on the wrong side of the tracks."

"Exactly, Major. Chakkri doesn't have a wealthy family nor the slightest trace of royalty in the old family tree. He's gone about as high as a guy from the wrong side of the tracks can go. Damn shame, too. He'd make one hell of a general."

Major Rama overheard the Americans' conversation but remained silent. The fact that they spoke so highly of his friend and commander was enough. No words were necessary. Arriving at the quarters that had been prepared for the visiting VIPs, Rama remained only long enough to see that they were adequate. They were more than acceptable. Ceiling fans sent a cooling breeze throughout the open-air living room which was furnished with a bamboo couch, a love seat with colorful plush cushions, and a variety of handsomely designed wicker chairs. Teakwood end tables stood beside each chair and the couch. A large teakwood dining table was centered in the room. Major Rama had reminded them of the time of the dinner party, then saluting, he departed. Ross, Jacoby, and the sergeant major gave the visitors a rundown on the day's training activities. After they had a chance to freshen up, they were encouraged to take a tour of the camp and the training facilities. Ross didn't believe in guided tours or preselected training that had been rehearsed for hours solely for the purpose of VIP visits. It showed the confidence the young captain had in his troops. They were all professionals, capable of handling any questions the two officers might have.

B.J. thanked them for the time they had taken from their busy schedule to meet them at the airport. Ross and his staff left the officers to the business of unpacking.

Jake pulled up one of the high-backed wicker chairs near a polished teakwood table and sat down as he said, "Ross and the boys seem like a pretty squared away bunch."

"Yeah," said B.J., as he walked across the room and opened the refrigerator, which stood in one corner of the room. It was filled with bottles of Budweiser beer, fruit, and a variety of different meats. Stepping to one side to allow his partner a view of the contents, he smiled as he said, "Yes, sir, Mr. Mortimer, this advisor business is a tough and dirty job, but somebody has to do it, and I guess we're elected. Just think, we're stuck with this for three whole weeks. Think we can handle it?"

Jake raised an open hand to catch the bottle of Bud that B.J. tossed to him. Twisting the cap off, he took a long drink of the ice-cold beer, then lowered the bottle onto the arm of the chair. Leaning back in the chair and placing his boots on the table, Jake Mortimer sighed as he said, "Yes sir, Mr. Mattson, three whole weeks of peace and quiet in a tropical paradise. Just goes to show you. Sometimes life can be a bitch."

CHAPTER 6

Kathryn Nickleson had detected the change in her husband's attitude after returning from her trip to Agra and the Taj Mahal. He had been irritable and moody all night. Attempts at trying to discuss what was wrong only seemed to irritate him even more. He had refused to talk to her about it, and she had decided it was best to drop the subject in the hope that by morning he would again be the fun loving, caring man he had been when they had begun this trip. Unfortunately, that was not the case. Even though Edward Nickleson was standing beside her, his mind was a million miles away. It was as if she were not even there. He had hardly said more than ten words all morning and now, as they waited to board the plane for Bangkok, he stood motionless, staring silently at Senator Kendell and his two security men as they came out of a room marked Senior Customs Inspector. The Thai customs official and Kendell were laughing as they and the security men, carrying two brown leather suitcases, walked past them and into the boarding tunnel that would take them to the plane. Kathryn saw her husband's face take on an angry, almost indignant appearance, as Kendell glanced their way in passing. It was a look she had never seen before.

"Edward, what's wrong? You're not acting like yourself."

Nickleson shook his head and, in a rough tone, spoke without bothering to look at her.

"I've already told you, Kathryn. There is nothing wrong. I wish you would stop asking the same question over and over again. It's becoming annoying."

"Well, excuse me, Edward. But you haven't exactly been mister sunshine yourself."

He stared down at her with a look that could have frozen water and started to say something back, but was interrupted by the return of the customs official who announced that they could now board the plane. Ignoring her, he walked away and hurried to get to the front of the line. He was determined to get a seat next to Kendell. This thing had become an obsession with him now, and he was not going to be denied some answers. Kathryn watched as he left her standing by herself. Tears were beginning to form in her brown eyes. An arm suddenly wrapped its way around her shoulders.

"Here, here, now," said Wanda Kendell. "We aren't having a little newlyweds' quarrel, are we?"

Kathryn had been so hurt by the way Edward had treated her that she could not find the words to answer.

Patting her on the arm, Mrs. Kendell began to walk her toward the entrance, all the time assuring her that lovers' quarrels were perfectly natural and added spice to a marriage. The making-up was always so much fun. Once inside, Wanda saw Nickleson and her husband at the rear of the plane. the bodyguards were standing on either side of them, and the discussion seemed to be a rather heated one. That was no place for Kathryn. The two lovebirds could get together after the men had finished their business. Finding two seats open near the front of the plane, Wanda pulled Kathryn in beside her and sat her near the window. "Never go to them, dear. Always make them come to you," she said as she lowered her plump frame into the seat next to Kathryn and smiled. "Don't you worry now, dear. He'll come begging once we're in the air. You'll see."

Kathryn Nickleson wasn't as sure and at the moment didn't really care. That haunting little voice that had tried to warn her about taking this trip had suddenly returned. It sent a cold chill down her back. Wanda Kendell was still talking, but she couldn't hear a word the woman was saying. Every nerve in her body seemed to be screaming for her to leap up and run from this plane—to get out any way she could. But what of Edward? He was already upset. Such an act now would only cause more trouble. What should she do? She turned toward the back of the plane, trying to get Edward's attention, but it was no use. He and the senator were deep in conversation. A stewardess interrupted and motioned for them to take their seats. They were about to take off. The sound of a heavy door shutting sent another chill through her as she swung her head back around in time to see the entrance door being closed and locked into place. The ever increasing roar of the engines, and the sudden movement of the plane as it began to roll onto the runway caused her entire body to tremble. Wanda gripped her hand tightly and pulled it to her huge breast, "Don't worry, dear. I'm right here. Everything will be just fine. We'll be in Thailand before you know it."

Kathryn Nickleson took in a deep breath and tried to convince herself that what the woman said was true. But somehow, deep within her very soul, she knew this time the voice was right.

Kendell fastened his seat belt and stared at Nickleson who now sat across from him, flanked by Alfonso and Rivera.

"I will say this only once more, Congressman. My affairs are none of your fucking business! Have I made that clear, Mr. Nickleson? I don't need a reason for my actions and I damn sure don't have to explain them to a freshman congressman from some small ass town in Iowa who was elected on the forgotten deeds of a dead hero father. As soon as we're airborne you'll return to your charming wife and stay the hell out of my section of this plane. If I have any more shit out of you, I'll have these two gorillas as you call them, throw your butt out of this plane. Believe me, Congressman. Mr. Rivera would like nothing better. Now that will be the end of this discussion."

Nickleson's face had gone bright red with anger. The veins in his neck were visibly pulsing as he fought to control himself. The remark about his father had sparked a reflex reaction. His fist was clenched, and he had started to rise out of the seat to pulverize the smirk from the senator's face. Only the strong grip of Alfonso and Rivera holding his shoulders had prevented him from smashing Kendell's face into hamburger.

"I don't know what you're up to, Senator, but I promise you, you'll regret the day you ever met me. You may have these others bullied and intimidated into looking the other way, but not me. My wife and I are leaving your little mystery flight in Bangkok. By the time you've finished whatever dirty business it is you're involved with, I, and a few people from the State Department, will be waiting for you when you land. If you won't talk to me, then I'm sure I can find somebody who will be just as interested in a couple of bags that had to be guarded by two thugs. Now call these dogs off me before I start screaming my brains out. And you know I'll do it."

If looks could kill, Nickleson would have already died a hundred times. The senator's hands were balled so tightly that his knuckles were turning white. His eyes were like two lasers of hate, burning holes through Nickleson. There was little doubt that the man would do just what he said he would do. Why had he even asked the son of a bitch to come on this trip? Wanda! He had put up with her harping for countless hours about inviting them until, in a moment of weakness, he had given in to her demands. Now he wanted to kill this freshman congressman, and he had two men with him that would be more than happy to do it. For a fleeting moment, the thought of including Mrs. Kendell in the same deal seemed more than a little inviting. No, that would be too hard to explain. Nickleson had no way of knowing what was really going on, but it was possible that once back in Washington, if he screamed loud enough and long enough, someone just might show enough interest to listen to his story. But who would believe him? There were a total of four senators and four congressmen on this trip, and their wives and staff. How was Nickleson going to convince anyone that out of all of these people traveling in the same group, he was the only one that saw Kendell involved in anything suspicious? They would laugh him out of Washington. He would be brought up before the Ethics Committee in the same week. No, Kendell didn't have to have him killed by two Mafia soldiers. He would take care of this young know-it-all himself and he was just the man that could get it done.

It was that kind of self-assured power that guaranteed him the backing of the others on this flight. To Kendell they were like the three monkeys that saw no evil, heard no evil, and especially, spoke no evil. Regaining his composure, the senator leaned back in his seat. A smirk distorted his face as he motioned for the two bodyguards to release Nickleson. Overhead, a soft bell tone sounded and the no smoking light went out as the plane reached cruising altitude. Without taking his eyes off him, the senator spoke in a calm, controlled tone.

"You're free to return to your own seat now, Congressman. Hopefully, by the time we reach Bangkok, you will have reconsidered your position and the possible consequences of any irrational actions or accusations on your part. I can assure you, Mr. Nickleson, that there are no hard feelings on my part. Should you reach the conclusion that perhaps this has all been a figment of your imagination, then I shall consider the matter closed and look forward to working with you in Washington."

Rivera and Alfonso seemed as shocked by the man's change of attitude as did the congressman. Nickleson wasn't buying it—and that was just what the senator was trying to do—buy him off. Rising to his feet, Nickleson stepped out into the aisle and leaned over Kendell.

"You know, Senator, I used to think we had a pretty good system in our country. Oh sure, it's not perfect; there's miles of red tape, tons of paper shuffling, and back room political bullshit deals; but you know, for all its faults, it's still the best system in the world. It's only when people like you take advantage of it that it really smells. I guess what

I'm trying to say is, you just gave me a choice between the system and looking the other way in order to stay on your good side." Nickleson leaned even closer. "Well, Senator, that isn't any choice at all. So fuck you!"

Rivera started to come out of his seat. Kendell waved him back down as Nickleson turned and walked away. The senator laid his head back and closed his eyes. He had offered the man a deal, and it had been turned down. So be it. He would not offer another.

Wanda Kendell, seeing Edward coming down the aisle, patted Kathryn's hand as she said, "Oh, here he comes. I told you he would. Now you just relax. We'll be in Thailand soon, and I'll take you to the cutest little shop that deals in gold. You'll just love it, I promise."

Nickleson stepped to one side to allow Wanda to pass. As she did so, she mentioned that Kathryn was having a difficult time on the flight. He nodded his thanks and moved to the seat she had vacated. Reaching for her hand, he smiled into her worried eyes and said, "Darling, I'm sorry I've been such a total ass today. It's not your fault. I'm afraid we're going to have to forego the elephant picture, Kathryn. Something has come up, and I need to get back to Washington as soon as possible. We'll be leaving the group in Bangkok and flying on home. I'm sorry, dear."

Her eyes still held a look of concern, but she managed a smile when he mentioned home.

"Oh, Edward, that is all I want. I don't care about Bangkok or elephants. I just want to be back in the safety of our home. Oh God! Please, just a little longer, please."

Nickleson gripped her hand tightly as he wrapped his arm around her and pulled her to him. "Kathryn, Kathryn, it's all right."

She was on the verge of hysteria now as she cried, "No, Edward, something is wrong. I can feel it. Oh Lord, please."

The head stewardess came quickly down the aisle.

"Is there a problem, sir?"

Kathryn's entire body was trembling now.

Nickleson didn't know what to do. Looking up at the

stewardess, he asked, "Do you have any type of tranquilizers aboard?"

"Yes, I'll get you some."

As the woman turned to go to the galley, the plane suddenly nosed forward, throwing the stewardess head first into the metal archway. A sickening crack was heard as her skull was split open from the impact. Magazines, books, briefcases, and people were tossed over seats and into the aisles. The plane nosed forward even more. They had lost all power and were going down fast. The force of the dive was crushing Nickleson back into his seat as he struggled to pull Kathryn back into hers. One minute she had been sitting beside him, the next second she had been thrown between the opening in the seats in front of them. Oxygen masks dropped from compartments above the seats. People were screaming. It was becoming hard to breathe. He was afraid to release his grip on Kathryn, but he had to have oxygen. Utilizing all the strength he had left, he leaned forward and jerked her free from the seats. Blood was coming from her nose, and there was a deep gash above her right eye that seemed to be pouring blood. Desperately, he grabbed for the mask above her seat and placed it over her face. Finding the seat belt, he wrapped it around her and pulled it tight. His vision was becoming blurred. The yellow mask swung back and forth in front of him. He reached out to grab it, but it kept swinging farther and farther away, until finally, it faded out from sight.

Major Randy York, the SOCOM communications officer, came out of the commo room and headed down the hall at a rapid gait. The expression of concern on his face caused those in the hall to pause and watch him as he passed. In his right hand he carried a manila folder with a red bordered cover sheet marked Top Secret.

General Sweet was conferring with his secretary in his outer office when he noticed York walking quickly past his door. He caught a glimpse of the classified document in the major's hand and noted the urgency in the man's stride. The secretary was asking Sweet a question, but he ignored her and moved to the doorway to see where the major was going in such a hurry.

York paused in front of General Johnson's office where he was met by Major Erin Hatch, the SOCOM intelligence officer. Both men conferred for a moment as York opened the folder, and Hatch read the communiqué. Judging from the look that came over Hatch's face, something very big had happened. Hatch closed the file and handed it back to York. Both conferred for a few more seconds, then disappeared inside Johnson's office.

Damn! Thought Sweet to himself, If Johnson hadn't found out about his informants in the communications section, he, not York, would have seen the message before anyone else. But now, Johnson had taken care of that. He had replaced every single man in the section, including the officers, with his own hand-picked crew, men that he knew were loyal to both him and to SOCOM.

"General, do you want these forms sent to both commands or only one?" asked the secretary.

"Wha—what?—Oh, never mind that now, Ms. Pringle. Please get Mr. Charles Burrows of the National Security Council on the line. I'll take the call in my office."

"Yes, sir," she replied as Raymond Sweet returned to his office, sat down in his overstuffed office chair, and waited for the return call. If anyone knew what was going on, it would be Burrows. He knew that General Johnson would eventually call him into his office and let him in on what had happened, but only after he and major Hatch had worked out a plan of action to deal with the situation—a plan of action that they were sure that he, Sweet, could not interfere with. They had snowed him on the Ecuadorian deal a few months ago, but it would not happen again. Burrows was right at the top. He would know exactly what was going on and what was in the communiqué that York had received. Johnson may have cut off his supply of information from his local informants, but he would be powerless against those in high places.

Charles Burrows was a man who, like many of the members of the Joint Chiefs, wanted to see SOCOM fall from grace and be disbanded. His reasons, however, were strictly personal. Burrows had done his three years in the military, but not as the flamboyant, Airborne Ranger, Green Beret, hard charging Rambo that he had envisioned himself to be. As a matter of fact, he had turned out to be more of a whimpering, complaining, Pee Wee Herman, who had used the influence of high-ranking friends of the family to get him through airborne school after failing not once, but four times. He had lasted less than a week at Ranger school, but had applied for Special Forces, again utilizing influence. Within a month he had been terminated from that course as well. Pressure by family and friends to reinstate him failed to sway the SF school's decision. He was out. Specialist Fourth Class Charles Burrows had spent his military service as a clerk typist in the finance office at Fort Bragg, North Carolina, where he had the unpleasant task of having to type up travel vouchers for the Airborne troopers, Rangers, and Green Berets that were drawing good money and traveling all over the world, doing all the things he had envisioned himself doing. Needless to say, there was little love lost between Burrows and SOCOM. He had gone to law school and had become involved in politics. Over the years he had worked himself up to his present position on the National Security Council. Sweet smiled to himself as he thought of these things. For those opposed to SOCOM, Charles Burrows was a man they could depend on.

The phone rang. Sweet answered, "Hello. General Sweet here."

"Raymond, this is Charles. I got your message. It was my understanding that you were not to call me unless it was absolutely necessary."

"Sorry, Charles, but I know something has happened and Johnson and his crew haven't let me in on it yet. I figured you could give me the straight scoop on what's happening. I don't want to be blindsided by these assholes again like I was during that Ecuador business. I'm sure you can understand that."

Sweet heard the heavy sigh on the other end of the phone as Burrows said, "Jesus, Raymond, I'm beginning to

wonder if having you down there isn't just a waste of time.
You mean you have no idea what is going on?"

Sweet hadn't expected that kind of remark from Burrows.
What did he mean by, "Having you down there is a waste
of time"? Hell, they couldn't be thinking of taking him out
of this assignment. He had just bought a condo, a boat, and
season tickets to all the Tampa Bay Bucs football games.

"Now wait a minute, Charles. I don't want you to think
I'm just fuc—"

Burrows cut him off. "Listen, Raymond, you had better
get yourself into Johnson's office—and I mean quick.
There's been a plane crash. A flight from New Delhi to
Thailand went down somewhere in the mountains of Burma
less than one hour ago. There were thirty-five Americans on
that plane, Raymond."

Sweet rocked back in his chair slowly as he said, "Okay.
So a plane crashes in Burma with some Americans aboard.
What's new about that? Hell, it happens all the time. Just
what makes this one so earth-shattering?"

There was a pause before Burrows answered. "General,
are you familiar with the name, Charles Kendell?"

The name brought Sweet straight up in his chair.

"You don't mean Senator Charles Kendell, do you?"

"Yes. Senator Kendell, his wife, and seven other senators
and congressmen were on that flight with their wives and a
staff of twenty-four people."

"My God," whispered Sweet. "Charles, do you realize
what could happen if the Communist insurgents running all
over Burma got their hands on any of those people,
especially Kendell?"

"Not only the guerrillas, General, but the drug warlords
as well. The man is chairman of the Drug Enforcement
Committee. I hate to even think of what they would want
for his return, or for any of them, as far as that goes. We had
hoped that the Burmese government would assist in the
location and rescue of any survivors, but no such luck. As
a matter of fact, they have banned any U.S. aircraft from
entering their air space. If we try it, they've sworn to shoot
them down. And of course we both know they have the

right to deny us use of their air space. Morally it sucks, but legally they've got us. The president cut off all aid to Burma after the military takeover in September of 1988. They haven't forgotten that, and you can bet your ass they will try to get to those people as soon as they can. I know I would. The president feels that General Saw Maung, who heads the place at the moment, will try to use the survivors as a bargaining chip to restore financial aid to his country."

"In other words, the bastard plans to blackmail us using Kendell and the others as hostages."

"That's the way we see it. Any action we take is going to have to be immediate. There is no time for massive alerts or organizing the necessary equipment and transportation to move large numbers of troops into position to call General Maung's bluff. Given the rugged conditions of the Burmese mountains and jungle, we figure that anyone that did survive can't last for long in that type of environment. Then, of course, there are the Communists, the drug boys, and the Burmese Army. That's why the president notified SOCOM. We need somebody that can get in there quick and get any survivors out of there before they become pawns in a political fiasco."

"Now, wait a minute, Charles. I thought we were supposed to be finding a way to get this outfit disbanded, not make them national heroes."

"General, I don't feel I should have to tell you your job. But if you can't find some way to make those people come out of this looking dirty, then perhaps we have sent the wrong man to sit in SOCOM headquarters." Burrows paused a moment for a response from Sweet. There was none. Obviously this was all happening too fast for him. Burrows realized he was going to have to give the man a push in the right direction to get him onto the idea he had in mind.

"My God, General, you have three prime ingredients in this situation, the Communists, the Burmese Army, and drug warlords." Burrows had emphasized the word drug. It was the key word that finally put Sweet on track.

"Drugs! We can let them pull off the rescue, then link

them somehow with trying to smuggle a supply of drugs back into the country. That should give us enough dirt to go around, wouldn't you say, Charles?"

Burrows tried to answer in a tone that would give Sweet the impression he had thought the idea up himself, but it was lacking in enthusiasm. "That's quite an idea you have there, Raymond. Can you manage it?"

"Of course I can. That's why you people chose me for this job. Don't worry about it, Charles. These overrated bozos are about to get their bubble burst. Thanks for filling me in on the details. I'll talk to you again when I'm in Washington. Good-bye, Charles."

"I know you can handle it, Raymond. Good luck."

Sweet had just replaced the phone on the receiver when there was a tap on his door and Major Hatch came into his office.

"General Sweet, sir. General Johnson would like all staff in the conference room in fifteen minutes. We are going to red alert."

Sweet faked a look of surprise as he asked, "Red alert? My, my, Major, what's going on?"

"Sorry, sir, I can't say right now. The general will explain the situation at the meeting."

"Very well, Major Hatch, fifteen minutes, in the conference room. I'll be there."

Hatch left as Sweet pulled open a drawer and removed two of his black-market, Cuban cigars from a box and placed one of them in his shirt pocket. Rolling the other in his chubby fingers for a moment, he brought it up to his mouth, bit off the tip, and spat it onto the floor as he sarcastically muttered, "The fuck you can't say, Major! Well, this time I'm ahead of you, and like the old saying goes, It's payback time."

CHAPTER 7

Mattson, Mortimer, and Major Rama were in one of the lookout towers near the main gate watching as a Thai native, perched on the back of an elephant, poked at a spot behind the animal's ear with a bamboo stick. The elephant responded by moving to the right and lowering his huge head, wrapped his long gray trunk around the end of a large log, and effortlessly picked it up. Another poke from the stick and the elephant lumbered its way across the corner of the compound, carrying the heavy log as if it were a toothpick curled tightly in his trunk.

"As you can see, Commander Mortimer," said Rama with a smile, "Even in this modern-day world of advanced technology, one of the earth's oldest inhabitants still provides a useful purpose. The elephant is used widely throughout my country for projects such as this. He is a creature that is both admired and respected in Thailand."

"I can see why," replied Jake.

Mattson was about to say something when his attention was drawn to the sound of an approaching helicopter. Major Rama and Jake both picked up the sound at the same time and turned to watch as the military chopper topped a mountain ridge and turned toward the camp.

"That is Colonel Decker's chopper," said Rama. "But I thought he was not arriving until later in the week."

"That's what he told us at the embassy a few days ago, Major," answered B.J.

Rama moved to the ladder beside the tower and swung his leg over the side. "You will please excuse me. I must alert Colonel Chakkri of Colonel Decker's arrival."

Jake watched, as Rama raced across the compound to Chakkri's quarters and went inside. "When we talked to Decker yesterday, he sure sounded like a man who wasn't planing on being here until the end of the week."

Mattson was already moving to the ladder as he answered, "You're right. Parsons had him scheduled for three days of staff meetings and social events. He wouldn't screw up that little man's time schedule unless something was wrong. We better get down there and see what's happened."

They went down the ladder and to the edge of the chopper pad that lay just outside the front gates. Chakkri and Rama joined them just as the skids of the bird touched down. There were four passengers on board. B.J. recognized Decker and Parsons, but not the two men with them.

Colonel Decker saluted Chakkri as the group approached.

"Sorry we didn't have time to get word to you that we were coming, Colonel. But we have a nasty situation on our hands and we're going to have to act fast if we expect to save the lives of a lot of people."

"Come, we will go to my headquarters and you can tell us what has happened," said Chakkri. "Major Rama, see to it that refreshments are brought to the conference room, then join us as soon as possible. Come this way, gentlemen."

Rama took off in a dead run for the mess hall while Chakkri led the group to his office. Decker fell in beside B.J. and Jake as they made their way across the compound, talking softly as they walked. "Man, am I glad you two guys are here. General Johnson says you are to take total control of this situation—says you're two of the best he's got."

"Sounds like our little vacation is over, Jake."

"It would seem that way, B.J. Colonel, what have we got?"

"It's bad, Jake, real bad. I don't mind telling you, I'm glad it's you guys that are going to be in charge and not me."

As they gathered around the table in the conference room, Decker caught Rama as he came into the room and whispered something to him. Rama left again and returned minutes later with a large, folded map, which he gave to Decker. B.J. noticed the harried look on the face of the timekeeper, Parsons. The two strangers next to him had the same look. As Decker unfolded the map and secured it to the wall, a corporal and two of the girls from the mess hall brought in trays containing ice-filled glasses and pitchers of tea and water. Placing then in the center of the table, they left the room, closing the door behind them. Chakkri motioned for the men to help themselves to the drinks. Marshall Parsons picked up a pitcher of tea and attempted to pour himself a glass, but his hand was shaking badly. One of the men next to him took the pitcher and filled the glass for him. Decker stepped to the front of the table and looked to Chakkri as if for approval to begin.

"Please begin, Colonel," said Chakkri as Major Rama sat down in the chair next to his commander.

Removing a telescopic metal pointer from his pocket, Decker extended it to its full length and began. "Gentlemen, first I would like to introduce the two men sitting next to Mr. Parsons. The gentleman on the right is Mr. Jason Talbut, former defense attache to Burma. Mr. Talbut has since retired from service, but lives here in Thailand and has offered us his services during this situation. He is very familiar with the Burma region, particularly the mountain areas. The gentleman to his right is Mr. Adam Lassiter. Mr. Lassiter is with the Central Intelligence Agency and has spent extensive time as a field operative and adviser to the Burmese Armed Forces and has knowledge of the terrain and the vast number of armed groups in the country. He will be going along on the operation with the ground team."

Jake shot B.J. a sideways glance when Decker mentioned the CIA. Lassiter didn't look old enough to be a CIA operative. The neatly cut blond hair and the blue-eyed, all-American boy look didn't seem to go with the CIA label. Especially the field operative part of the statement. B.J. figured that Lassiter was younger than Mortimer, which would rule out any possibility that the kid had seen action in Vietnam. If he were going by looks, B.J. would have figured Talbut to be the CIA man. With pepper-speckled hair and a weathered face that showed both the experience and cunning that would be expected of an American intelligence man, he was more Parson's age. B.J. directed his attention back to Decker, who had now turned to the map on the wall.

"Gentlemen, at 0800 hours this morning a special airline passenger plane departed New Delhi, India with forty people aboard and a crew of seven. Its destination was Bangkok. At approximately 1115 hours that plane radioed a distress call that was picked up by the Mingaladon Airport in Burma as well as the Chiang Mai Airport here in Thailand. The crew radioed that they had lost all power and were losing altitude. Things must have been pretty hectic up there because the one thing they didn't tell us was their position. Chiang Mai tower tried for fifteen minutes to reestablish contact with the aircraft, but they were unsuccessful." Turning to the map, Decker placed the tip of the pointer on the spot marked New Delhi and began to move it slowly across India, then to Bangladesh and across the border of Burma.

"We have charted the approximate air speed, time, and distance. Our experts believe that the plane went down in the northern portion of the Shan Plateau, in what they call the Shan State. It is extremely rough, mountainous country with steep slopes and heavy jungle. The odds that the crew could have made even a half-assed safe landing are about zero to none."

As Decker turned away from the map and paused for a moment, Jake asked, "Major, have the Burmese launched any type of spotter or rescue aircraft?"

"We have no way of knowing, Commander," replied Decker flatly.

Mortimer seemed surprised. "Excuse me, sir, but I thought we had an embassy in Burma."

"We do, Jake. But after General Maung pulled off his military takeover last September, our government cut off all aid to Burma. Needless to say, it wasn't long after that, that they kicked us out of the country and advised any Americans living there to get out while they could. In effect, we're in the dark as to what actions the Burmese are taking in this situation. The CIA still has valuable inside agents within the government, but it will be days before we can get any information from them. We just don't have the time to wait."

B.J. saw Parsons glancing nervously at his watch. Beads of sweat had formed on the little man's forehead. Looking back at Decker, he said, "Major, I get the feeling that with the CIA and SOCOM involved in this thing and Mr. Parsons about to have an anxiety attack, that we are not talking about a simple plane crash with your everyday, Mr. and Mrs. John Doe aboard."

"You're absolutely right, B.J. That special flight out of New Delhi was carrying a congressional party headed by Senator Charles Kendell. There were four senators, four congressmen, their wives, and a staff of twenty-four on board."

"Holy shit!" exclaimed B.J.

Colonel Chakkri rose to his feet and stepped to the map. "That is actually an appropriate statement Major Mattson," he said as he tapped his finger in the area believed to be the crash site. "I can not attest to the religious accuracy, but I can tell you that if this is the area in which the plane crashed, then they are truly in the shit—and up to their necks, I might add."

Decker nodded in agreement, and B.J. thought he heard a low moan come from Marshall Parsons.

"You see, Major," continued Chakkri, "this particular area is a hotbed of armed activity."

"Communist insurgents?" asked Jake.

"Buddha could possibly smile upon them if that were the only problem, Commander. I am afraid any of your surviving government officials may find themselves wishing they had died in the crash. If they are fortunate, they will be found by the Communist guerrillas, perhaps even the Shan Revolutionary Army. However, should Buddha turn away from them, their fate could well rest in the hands of some of that country's most notorious gangsters and renegades. These hills are infested with revolutionaries; renegade Chinese army deserters; drug warlords, who have whole armies that rule over the towns and villages; and of course, mountain bandits, well-armed groups of cutthroats made up from the scum and sewer filth of Southeast Asia. They do battle with anyone and everyone that gets in their way; Communists, warlords, government troops, it doesn't matter to them. They burn, rape, and destroy everything in their path for the sheer joy of something to do because they know no other way of life. I need not tell you the fate that awaits the American women that may have survived this crash, should they be found by these barbarians. So you see, no matter who may find them, getting them back will be no easy task."

Visions of the fate of the women turned Parsons's face an ashen gray.

Colonel Chakkri returned to his seat as B.J. said, "Thank you, Colonel. Okay, Major Decker, Jake and I have the picture now. It is obvious that time is going to be a major factor in this situation. Those people won't last long out there. If the crash didn't get them, the jungle or one of those gun crazy groups running around in there will. It doesn't sound like a Mr. Rogers type of neighborhood."

Decker turned to Parsons. "Marshall, you were with the ambassador at the embassy when the message came in from the White House. Why don't you handle this part."

Parsons swallowed down the remaining tea in his glass before standing and moving to the front of the room. The little man was a whiz at organizing and timetables, but those were material things and projections. This was totally different. People's lives were at stake. Those in the room could tell Parsons was uncomfortable about being involved.

"Ttthhe—" His voice had cracked. Coughing once, he began again.

"The president of the United States was informed of the situation less than two hours ago. He immediately established contact with General Saw Maung, the ruling military leader of Burma, requesting assistance in the location and rescue of our people. Maung however, sees this as an opportunity to reinstate the massive foreign aid that was cut off after his coup of last year. He has made demands of the president that are both ridiculous and totally unacceptable. Appeals for assistance for moral and humanitarian reasons have fallen on deaf ears. General Maung has stated that until his demands are met, the borders and air space over Burma are closed to the United States. Any violation of this order by America will be considered an act of war and will result in the arrest and imprisonment of the four to five hundred priests, missionaries, and various church groups that have remained in Burma."

B.J. shifted slightly in his chair as he shook his head and said, "We could have another Iranian hostage situation if that happened."

"Exactly, Major Mattson," replied Parsons, "and the president has no desire to become caught up in another fiasco like that. Maung is desperate. He made a lot of promises to the Burmese people when he took over and without our financial aid, he is finding it impossible to keep those promises. The people are becoming restless, and that has him worried. There has already been an ever increasing number of riots in the cities. This may be the general's last hope of reestablishing the financial assistance he needs to maintain power in the country."

"Okay, General Maung is willing to let us come in and save our own people for a price, but we're not willing to pay that price because with a vault full of money the son of a bitch could stay in power forever, and the Burmese would never get their country back from the military. Is that about it?" asked Mattson.

"Well, yes, Major." said Parsons. "Roughly put, but factual."

"That's what I figured. So while over thirty Americans are lying out in that jungle either dead, dying, hurt, or scared to death, we are still playing the damn politics game. Screw this fucking General Maung! Let's just go get our people."

Lassiter smiled across the table at Mattson. The young CIA man had said exactly the same thing at the embassy less than one hour ago.

"That is why we are here, Major Mattson," said Lassiter, still smiling. "General Johnson at SOCOM says that you and Commander Mortimer are two of the best he has. If anybody could get in there and bring those people out, it was the M & M boys."

Jake was smiling now. He knew how B.J. hated that term.

"Well now, ain't that special? He didn't happen to send along an operations plan with all that confidence, did he?" asked B.J.

"No, afraid not, Major. He did say, however, that with time being a factor, you were authorized to use Colonel Decker's 75th Rangers for mounting an immediate plan of operation."

Mattson looked across at Decker who nodded his approval as he said,

"You've had a few days to watch my boys in action, B.J. I think they can handle it."

"Mr. Lassiter, since I am certain your agency has been in contact with the royal family about this matter, would you mind letting me know what part my command and I are to play in this situation?" asked Chakkri.

Lassiter glanced up at Parsons who nodded his approval.

"Yes, sir, you are correct. The king has been informed and has consented to allow us to launch our mission from here. However, for obvious political reasons, neither you nor your troops are to be involved in the cross-border operation itself. You may establish artillery support positions along the northern border area to provide cover fire for the extraction should it become necessary, but under no circumstances are you to cross the border with an armed force."

Neither Chakkri nor Major Rama appeared pleased with the king's decision. They would have preferred to join forces with the Americans for the ground operation, but both were loyal Thai officers and would honor the king's orders. Jake and B.J. were equally disappointed at the news. The Thais would have given them a vital edge on the ground, not that they didn't have confidence in Decker's Rangers. They were all hard charging young troopers in top physical condition, but the only combat that most of them had seen had been in Grenada, and that was nothing compared to where they would be going this time. It would be a bunch of young, inexperienced kids up against hard-core, experienced Asian jungle fighters and mercenaries. A lot of them would not be coming back.

Parsons removed his watch from his pocket and stared at it in silence as a reminder to the others that time was still very much a factor.

Mattson was the first to rise. "Well, gentlemen, the task lies before us. Colonel Decker, I would suggest that we notify your platoon sergeants to gather the command in one of the training areas, and let them in on our plans. Mister Parsons, within the next couple of hours we will have a compiled list of special equipment and supplies that we will need for the operation. I trust that you have the connections and the pull to get us whatever we may need in this emergency?"

Parsons nodded in the affirmative as he replied, "You need only to ask, Major, and you'll have it."

"Fine. Then, Jake, I want you and Mr. Lassiter to get me the latest intelligence on the crash area and what particular group of assholes we are most likely to encounter once we're in there. Colonel Decker, how many medics do you have with your Rangers?"

"Six MOS qualified and five cross-trained."

"That's good. We're going to need every one of them. Colonel Chakkri, sir, I would appreciate it if you and Major Rama would work with Commander Mortimer and Mr.

Lassiter on the intelligence update and map study. We are going to need some aircraft for this thing; either rotored or fixed wing, depending on what kind of an infiltration plan we come up with. Jake, I'll be in the communications section. I want to get in touch with General Johnson and see what is going on back there." Mattson paused for a moment to consider if he had missed anything. He didn't think so.

"Okay, gentlemen, that's it. Let's get with it. Somewhere out there are a lot of scared people and we're the only hope they've got," said B.J. as he headed for the door. Lassiter and Jake were standing beside the map as the room began to clear.

"Your partner seems to be a natural at this business," said Lassiter.

"Yeah, he is. This is his kind of environment, and you won't find many that are any better at it. Too bad Charlotte doesn't understand that."

"Who?" asked Lassiter.

Jake hadn't meant to bring her name up in all this; it just slipped out.

"Oh, nothing. Guess I had my mind someplace else." Jake turned away from Lassiter and faced the map as he asked, "When was the last time you made a jump, Mr. Lassiter?"

Jake noted the slight rise in the young CIA agent's voice as he replied, "Uh—about seven or eight months ago. Why?"

"Because that's the only way we're going to get in there in time to do those people any good. Was that last jump of yours static line or HALO?"

"It—it was static line. A refresher jump at the Farm in Virginia. I haven't done free-fall in—in over a year. Can't we get in there without doing a high altitude low opening jump?" It sounded more like Lassiter was pleading than asking a question. That surprised Jake. A guy didn't get to be a CIA field operative unless he had a pair of balls the size of King Kong and a gung-ho attitude that would put John Wayne to shame.

"You have a problem with free-fall?" asked Jake.

"No—no problem, Commander." Lassiter lowered his eyes as he half mumbled, "I'm just not very good at it. Especially at night. The last one I did was a training jump with some guys from the Delta Force. It was a night drop at ten thousand feet. Somehow I lost them in the fall and got separated. They landed around the target and I landed in a damn reservoir for a sewage treatment plant. God, the smell was terrible. Like to have never got out of that thing."

Jake couldn't help but laugh as he placed his hand on the man's shoulder and said, "Well now, that's an interesting story, Lassiter, and I want to tell you that it gives me great confidence to know I'll be working with a guy that's been in the shit."

A smile broke across the young man's face as he, too, began to laugh.

"Well, obviously I didn't learn anything from that experience, Commander."

"What do you mean?" asked Jake.

Lassiter reached up and tapped the map in the square that had been designated as the possible crash site.

"It would appear that I am about to jump into the shit again."

Both men were laughing as Colonel Chakkri and Major Rama came into the room with a stack of folders and another large map. The two Thai officers looked at each other as if they were trying to figure out just what could be so funny considering the situation. Colonel Chakkri simply shrugged his shoulders and shook his head. He had never quite mastered the logic of the American sense of humor; he doubted he ever would.

Having completed his short conversation with General Johnson, B.J. returned to the conference room that had now become an operations center. A larger, more detailed map had now joined the smaller one on the wall. Various colored markings identified the different enemy forces and their last know locations. Two of the colors appeared more prominent among the colors on the map. The blue signified the forces of General Chin Tu Ling, a Chinese drug warlord, who apparently held vast territories in the mountain ranges around the suspected crash sight. The other color that stood out was a dull brown, this one signifying the forces of a mountain bandit known as Yang Hwe Kang; he was also Chinese and was reported to have an army equal to that of General Ling. His headquarters or base of operations was believed to be located less than ten miles from where the plane had gone down.

Seeing the solemn look on B.J.'s face as he studied the multicolored map, Jake closed the folder he was reading and joined his partner at the board.

"What did the ol' man have to say?"

"Plenty. Washington is jumping out of their ass. The House and Senate have called an emergency meeting of the intelligence committee, and the Joint Chiefs of Staff are screaming for immediate military action, and this time they might just get what they want. There are plenty of politicians agreeing with them, and the numbers keep getting larger as the screaming gets louder. You see, Jake, there's a difference here. If these were just your everyday Mr. and Mrs. U.S. Citizen, they'd be drag assing around saying how they had to be cautious about committing troops and that negotiating was the only way to handle this, but let it happen to some of their people and they're ready to stage a fucking Normandy Invasion and screw the consequences. It's enough to make me want to puke. They'll do all the screaming and we'll be the ones that do the dying."

"Yeah, it's a hell of a business, that's for sure. Makes a fellow wonder why he stays with it, doesn't it? Why he'd expect his wife and family to understand this shit when he doesn't even understand it himself. Yeah, I guess that's why old assholes like you stay around just to show us younger assholes how sick the business really is. Couldn't possibly be because you think you're accomplishing something for your country and your fellow countrymen, no matter how unappreciative they may be from time to time."

Mattson, with a slight smile at the edges of his mouth, turned his eyes away from the map and looked at Jake. "Guess I was starting on one of those self-pity, Holy Roller kicks again, huh?"

Jake was grinning as he replied, "Well, let's just say you were at a point where if I had to make a choice between listening to that bullshit or sticking a finger down my throat, the finger would win out. Either way, I would get the same results, and somebody would have to clean up the floor. So what other delightful news did the general have for us?"

"You'll love this. General Johnson will be here within twenty-four hours."

"I've got no problem with that."

"Me, either. But would you like one guess at who else is coming along?"

A disappointed look spread over Jake's face as he sighed, "No, don't tell me he's bringing our favorite boy along."

"You got it. The ol' man said he tried to get out of it, but Sweet has some pretty strong pull somewhere up the line. He'll be here tomorrow."

Turning back to the map, Jake tapped the quadrangle that had been blocked off in red as he said, "Damn. You know it's a crying shame when you'd rather be out there in the shit than around another officer. Well, let's get something put together here and go to work before that dick arrives and has a chance to screw it up. Jesus, I hate this shit."

Jake turned back to B.J. in time to see him bring his finger up to his mouth and make a move as if he were shoving it down his throat.

"Is this how we do it?" asked B.J.

"Ah, fuck you, B.J." said Jake as they both laughed out loud.

Colonel Chakkri glanced up at the two Americans then back at the pad on which he had written a list of numbers. He didn't know what the two men had found to laugh about. If his figures were correct, they would be facing an army of close to one thousand under the command of General Ling and anywhere from six to eight hundred under the command of the bandit leader, Kang. Colonel Chakkri could find little humor in those odds. But then again, these were not just ordinary soldiers, nor ordinary men.

Major Decker, Captain Ross, and the 160-man contingent that was B Company of the 75th Rangers, listened intently from the bleachers as Major Mattson explained the situation and the importance of time factors. Jake stood next to an easel that held the charts showing the operations plan and the team breakdown by names and sections for the rescue mission. Jake allowed his eyes to roam each row of the bleachers as he studied the faces of the Rangers. Although there were a few older faces among the crowd, most seemed so young. That fact could be attributed to the rigorous physical demands of the Ranger school at Fort Benning, Georgia, where only six out of every twenty that volunteered made the grade. The training was long and exhausting, with men going for three days and nights carrying sixty to seventy pounds on their backs and covering nearly fifty miles, often with only two hours' sleep squeezed in at ten- or fifteen-minute intervals during the three days. It was not a course for one who lacked the confidence, the drive, and the motivation to excel at his full potential. You didn't fake your way through Ranger school. You could either cut it or you couldn't; there was no middle ground. For those that faltered in this quest there were other assignments to go on to, with the chance to come back at a later date to give it another try. However, for those that met the challenges head-on and endured, there was the sacred gold Ranger tab affixed above the unit patch on their left shoulder. It signified more than just the completion of a school; it signified the character of the man who wore it. There were 160 such men now sitting in front of Jake Mortimer.

B.J. Mattson saw no reason to sugarcoat the task that lay before them. Maybe if it had been an upcoming football game with an old rival, or a basketball game, but those were only kids' games, where, if you lost, you went home and tried again next year. Not so in this business. Here, there were no kids. In this game, if you lost, you came home in a body bag. There were no rematches.

Jake removed the cards one at a time as B.J. proceeded through the briefing. The men in front of him kept their eyes riveted on each chart and their minds on every word spoken by Mattson. Captain Ross had been right; they were every bit as sharp as he had said they were. Regrettably, some of them would not be alive by this time tomorrow. Mattson concluded the briefing by saying, "There you have it, gentlemen. Beyond those mountains and in that jungle are a group of frightened Americans, hurt and alone. We are their only hope. Are the Rangers capable of the monumental task that awaits them?"

The air around the training site filled with a resounding roar, screamed in unison, "Yessssss! Airborne! Ranger!"

Mattson beamed with pride at their answer.

"All right, then, platoon leaders and platoon sergeants, conduct your weapons checks and equipment distribution. Be prepared to move out in one hour. Let's go kick some ass, Rangers!"

Another wild cheer erupted as B.J. and Jake headed for the conference room for one final check of their battle plan and any new intelligence information that may have come in over the wire.

There was nothing fancy nor unique about the rescue plan. Time did not allow for elaborate layouts and rehearsals for infiltration or actions at the objective. These were all basic things that the Rangers had gone through during those long, torturous days and weeks at the school. B.J. could only hope that they had learned their lessons well. Their very lives, as well as the lives of those with them, would depend on that.

In one hour the entire group would move to the far side of the Chiang Mai airport, the military side. During the initial planning it was necessary to find out how many of the 160-man Ranger unit were HALO (High Altitude Low Opening) qualified. Jumping out of a perfectly good airplane at two or three thousand feet was one thing, but a night drop from fifteen thousand feet, with full combat equipment, was another thing altogether. B.J. had hoped at least half of the company would be qualified, but had to settle for less than that. All 160 had volunteered, but only 60 met the requirements. Among them, were three old-time platoon sergeants who had seen action in both Vietnam and Grenada. B.J. considered that a plus. He and the 60 skydivers would depart Chiang Mai aboard a C-130 aircraft. Once over the suspected crash site at an altitude of fifteen thousand feet, B.J., Lieutenant Jacoby, and 28 of the men would exit first. Captain Ross and Jake would hold the remainder of the men for approximately ten seconds, then they would exit the aircraft. This would give the Rangers a wide area of distribution in which to conduct their search. Once on the ground, the two groups would confirm their location and establish radio contact between themselves and Lieutenant Colonel Decker, who, with Colonel Chakkri and the remainder of the Rangers, would establish a base of operations at the border outpost located north of the village of Chiang Rai. Decker's force would serve as the RDF (Rapid Deployment Force). A total of seven unmarked helicopters consisting of four MH-53 Pave Lows and three UH-60 Blackhawks had been provided by the king of Thailand for the rescue effort. If their estimate of the crash site was correct, the plane had gone down in Burmese territory, thirty miles north-northwest of the Thai border outpost. B.J. would be located to the west of the quadrangle, while Jake and his group would be on the east side. They would begin a sweeping search pattern, moving forward after each sweep until they linked up in the center of the quad. Should they encounter hostile forces, they were to attempt to break contact, lay low until the area was clear, and then continue the search. Should the contact reach a terminal stage, the group not engaged would abandon the search and move with all haste to the assistance of the group under attack. Should that fail and the entire mission become terminal, Decker and the RDF force would be airlifted into the battle area to provided assistance in securing the area for the evacuation of the wounded and all survivors. If all went well, this action would not be required; but if it became necessary, they all hoped it wouldn't come until after they had located the downed aircraft. Otherwise, they would have no choice but to inform Washington that they had tried and failed.

This was a mission for which it would normally take a unit of experienced combat troops a month to prepare; they had done it in four hours. Less than twenty percent of their force had any combat experience at all. Throw in the Murphy's Law principle, which states that if anything can go wrong, it will, and you had all the ingredients for a prime-time disaster. But other than that, it was going to be nothing more than another day at the office for those who played this deadly game.

Jake and Colonel Chakkri had gone to the communications room to coordinate the movement of some heavy artillery pieces to the border outpost. They might not need it, but B.J. wanted it on call just the same. They were going to need every edge they could get on this one. B.J. was studying the map as Adam Lassiter came over to him, holding two cups of coffee. Extending one to B.J., he said, "Thought you might like some. It's fresh made."

"Thanks, Mr. Lassiter."

"Please, let's drop the mister, stuff, okay? The name's Adam."

"Okay," said B.J., as he took a sip of the hot coffee and smiled at the young CIA man, at least thirteen years his junior.

"Been with the agency long, Mr. Lass . . . I mean Adam?"

"Four years, now, Major."

Mattson raised his hand. "B.J."

"Four years . . . B.J."

"Well, Adam, I hope you'll excuse me, but you seem awfully young to be in that line of work. What made you pick the CIA?"

"One of those family traditions, I guess. My dad was in the OSS with Wild Bill Donovan back in World War II. Dad's retired now; he spent nearly his whole life working the spy business. We used to go for long walks when he was home, which wasn't really all that often, but he'd need somebody to talk to. Guess I was lucky there. I wasn't just his son; I was his best friend, too. He felt that there was nothing he couldn't talk to me about. So, when he'd come home, we'd talk about where he had been and what had happened; sometimes it was good, other times the mission had turned out bad and he'd blame himself for something not going right. Sometimes he'd even break down and cry when he lost old friends on an operation. He's quite a fellow, my old man. Always honest, straightforward, and not afraid to show emotion. They were qualities I admired in him as my father and as a man. The agency had helped build that in him, and I wanted to be just like my old man, so here I am."

Mattson's respect for the young man had just jumped a hundred points. B.J. wondered if his son ever felt that way about him. He hoped that some day his son would talk about his father as eloquently as this man had done.

"Have you seen much combat, Adam?" asked B.J.

"I've spent a little time in Angola against the Cubans, and I had a few months in Afghanistan trading shots with the Russians."

B.J. was smiling again. He liked this kid. "Well, that resume definitely qualifies you for our little party. The terrain will be rough, steep hills and thick jungle, easy to get turned around and disorientated in. Since you've worked in there before and know the area, you'll be a big help to us."

"Whatever you say, Maj—I mean, B.J. You're the head honcho on this thing. It's a job I don't envy you, either."

They were joined by Jason Talbut who had just come into the room. The elderly man stared at the red blocked quadrangle for a moment, then sighed as he said, "God, to be twenty years younger. I'd love to be going in there with you guys."

Mattson placed his hand on Talbut's shoulder as he replied, "If that were the case Mr. Talbut, I would willingly relinquish command and be more than happy to follow you in there. The information about the area that you have provided us could well mean the difference between pulling this thing off or losing all those people. You've been a great help to us, sir, and we thank you."

Talbut tried to hide the appreciation he felt for Mattson's words. It had been a long time since he had received such high praise.

"Well, I might not be able to go in there with you, but Colonel Decker has consented to let me fly up to that border outpost with them so I can listen in on the action."

"That's fine, Mr. Talbut. We can use all the moral support we can get and a few prayers wouldn't hurt, either."

Jake entered the room and said, "B.J., Parsons just called. The parachutes and the other equipment just arrived at the hangar. The pilots and the aircraft are ready whenever we are." Jake paused a moment, and a disheartened look came over him as he continued. "There's one other thing— He said the news people have broken the story about the plane going down. They were supposed to give us a twenty-four-hour blackout, but I guess somebody figured they could improve their ratings. They just had it on CNN news; he thought we should know."

B.J. nodded. There was nothing he could say that would change it. The minute that story hit the screen, they had lost a valuable edge in their race against the clock. Now, not only did the people in the immediate area know about the downed airliner, but so did every fanatical group in the country. He had hoped they could get in and out before the whole world knew about it. Now that advantage had been taken away. A simple little thing like a ratings game between rival television networks had just doubled the odds that twice as many Rangers were going to die in the next twenty-four hours, but the networks wouldn't look at it that way. They never did.

CHAPTER 8

Ignoring the sharp pain that shot through his neck, Edward Nickleson moved his head slightly to one side and tried to open his eyes. Somewhere in the background he could hear the whimpers of a woman crying and the painful moans of a man somewhere close to him. His head was pounding and his entire body seemed to ache, especially his back. He was lying on something hard that pressed into his spine. It felt like the arm of one of the seats. He tried to move off the object, but the attempt sent a jolting shock of pain throughout his body. Something heavy was pressing down on his chest, restricting his efforts. Opening his eyes slowly, he tried to focus his blurred vision on the object above him. It was bright green and seemed to have a web of twisting, turning legs. Blinking his eyes a few times to clear them, he saw the lush green vines of the jungle protruding through a huge hole in the top of the airplane. The heavy smell of fuel hung in the air. Kathryn? Where was Kathryn? He had placed her oxygen mask over her face. That was the last thing he could remember. He had to find her.

Nickleson tried again to force himself off the object in his back, but the weight on top of him held him down. At the angle he was lying, he could move his head to the left and right; however, the weight on his chest and the bottom frame of one of the seats hanging less than an inch above his forehead prevented him from raising his head. Pulling an arm free from under his hip, he brought his hand up and searched blindly for whatever was holding him down. His hand came to rest on a piece of fabric. Feeling along the object, he realized that it was a man's body across his chest. Moving his hand farther up the back, he suddenly stopped. He felt something wet and sticky on his hand. Bringing it up slowly in front of his face, he saw the bright red color of blood covering his hand all the way to the wrist. "Oh, God," he groaned, as he began to panic. The thought of Kathryn lying helpless and bleeding sent a surge of adrenaline firing through him. With near superhuman strength, he brought his hand to the edge of the overhanging seat and with one mighty shove, pushed the bent metal structure straight up and away from him. Raising his head and looking down at his chest, he was not prepared for the sight he saw before him. The body was that of the man from Florida, Congressman Meeker—or at least he thought it was; there was no way to tell for sure. There was only a pool of blood where the man's head should be. Terrified by the sight, he jerked his other arm free and pushed, punched, and shoved, until he had moved the decapitated body off him. Pulling himself up onto his knees, he saw the total destruction that lay all around him. Seats, cushions, metal trays, and briefcases were scattered everywhere and among them lay the broken and shattered bodies of the passengers. Looking to the rear of the plane where Senator Kendell had been sitting, Nickleson saw that the tail section had been torn off, and what remained of the plane appeared to be a giant archway that led into the jungle beyond. For the first time he felt the steamy heat that filled the plane. The heat, the strong fumes from the fuel tanks, and the sickening smell of blood that drenched his shirt and pants caused Nickleson to double over and vomit.

Congressman Thomas Howell had dug himself out from beneath the crumpled seats and twisted metal that had been the port windows. Seeing Nickleson, he cradled his shattered right arm with his left and edged himself slowly through the debris. It was as if he were walking through hell. Bodies covered in blood lay everywhere. One of the young women on the staff sat perfectly upright in one of the few seats that had not been torn from the flooring. Her seat belt was still tightened firmly around her waist, her head was tilted back, and her lifeless eyes stared up through the hole in the top of the plane. A metal arm from one of the chairs behind her had slammed into the back of her seat with a terrific force and now protruded a full six inches from her chest. Howell, like Nickleson, was overcome by an attack of nausea.

Nickleson slowly raised his head, his face covered with sweat. Seeing Howell gave him a spark of hope that there were more people still alive. Struggling to ignore the headless body that lay at his feet, he began to pull the loose cushions and debris from around the area where he and Kathryn had been sitting. It was not until he tore away a section of the overhead compartment that had collapsed onto the seats that he found her. Her face was covered in blood from the cut she had received when the plane had initially nose-dived. There was a small bump above her left eye, but other than that she appeared to be all right. There were no broken bones that he could see. The fuel odor seemed to be getting stronger. He had to get her out into the air and away from the wreck. Slowly picking her up in his arms, he maneuvered his way to a side door that had sprung open. Stepping over the body of a woman lying in front of the door, he recognized her as the one who had offered to get Kathryn the tranquilizers. She was dead.

Carrying his wife a safe distance away from the plane, Nickleson placed her gently on the ground near a small stream that flowed from an outcropping of jagged rocks. Pulling his shirt off, he tore away the bloodied portion and threw it away. Soaking the other half in the cold, running water, he bent down and began to wash the dried blood from Kathryn's face. Her head moved first; slowly the eyes opened, and she stared up at him. Tears began to form, then overflow to run down her bloodstained cheeks. She tried to speak, but he placed his finger to her lips and shook his head as he whispered, "No. That's all right, darling. Just rest for a while. We don't need to talk right now. I'm all right, and you're going to be fine. We made it."

Kathryn managed a meager smile as she closed her eyes again. Howell eased himself down through the doorway and made his way over to Nickleson. It was clear that the middle-aged congressman was in pain from the shattered arm as he asked, "Is she all right, Edward?"

"Yes, Thomas, thank God. How about your wife?"

Howell looked away and up at the towering jungle canopy that hung high above them. "She's dead. Broken neck, I think. Martha always did complain about her neck, you know. Funny, I can't seem to remember the last time I told her I—I—"

Howell's voice trailed off and he was silent as he walked away. Other survivors began to make their way out of the shattered hulk of the plane. There were more than Nickleson had believed possible. The initial shock of their ordeal had worn off, and now, those who were able began to help remove the injured from the tangled wreckage inside. Nickleson was surprised to see Wanda Kendell come stumbling out of the jungle brush a few feet away. She was staggering from side to side. A thin line of blood ran down one side of her neck from a cut along her right ear. Her skirt was ripped and her blouse was torn on one side, exposing a huge bare breast that had come free from her broken bra strap. Nickleson could tell by the dazed look in her eyes that she had no idea where she was. Leaving Kathryn's side, he removed a coat that had been placed over the face of one of the dead and walked over to Mrs. Kendell. Placing the coat around her shoulders, he led her to where Kathryn was lying and had her sit down; then eased her back against a tree trunk.

"Mrs. Kendell, what about your husband and the others?"

Wanda Kendell smiled a silly grin and cocked her head to one side. "He's a senator, you know. My husband is a senator."

Nickleson could see the woman was still in a state of shock. He wouldn't get any information from her. Karen

Newell, wife of the Pennsylvania congressman, saw him kneeling at Kathryn's side and joined him.

"How is she, Edward?" she asked.

"She took a bad bump on the head, Karen, but I think she'll be all right. How about your husband?"

"He's okay. A few scrapes and bruises, but nothing serious. We were both very lucky. He'd helping the others out now. How about Wanda?"

Nickleson stood up as he said, "Shock, but nothing serious. Listen, Karen, would you mind staying with them for a few minutes? I want to see if I can find Senator Kendell. He was in the section of the aircraft that broke off at the tail. Wanda came wandering out of the jungle back there. I want to check it out."

"Of course, Edward. You go ahead. I'll be here if she comes out of it."

"Thanks, Karen," he said as he turned and walked to the point at the edge of the thick jungle from which he had seen Wanda exit. Pushing his way into the lush growth, he had gone a hundred feet into the jungle when he heard a low mournful cry coming from somewhere to his left. He changed directions and rapidly covered the short distance to the point where he had heard the sound. Pulling back a thick group of low hanging vines, he saw the missing tail section. The bodies of two men and a woman lay a few feet from the open end of the tail. It was obvious that they were all dead. The bodies were twisted and contorted in sickening positions.

Nickleson picked up the faint sound of the moan again and moved to the side of the wreckage. The man, Rivera, sat propped against the side of the metal structure. His face was an ashen gray color and the fingers of his two hands were interlocked. They were pressed tightly against his stomach. Small streams of blood oozed between his fingers and down the backs of his hands. Rivera's glazed eyes looked at Nickleson, begging for help.

"He's had it, Congressman. Don't need to waste your time. Piece of that metal there caught him across the gut—opened him up like you'd gut a fish." Nickleson turned to see the giant, Alfonso, standing at the end of the tail section. His shirt was torn and there was a deep gash down his left arm that had been bound by a piece of shredded material. Nickleson gave the man a disgusted look, then knelt down to see if he could do anything for Rivera. The Mexican's upper lip quivered as the congressman tried to get him to move his hands out of the way so he could survey the damage.

"No—no, senõr, please, my guts, they will spill out onto the ground if I remove my hands. My—in my pocket, my inside coat pocket, the small bag—that is all I will need, please, senõr."

Nickleson reached into the coat and removed the small bag Rivera had asked for. Opening it, he found it filled with a white powder. Rivera nodded, and, on the verge of tears, cried, "Please, senõr. My mouth—pour it in my mouth."

Nickleson looked over at Alfonso who shrugged his shoulders and said, "Go ahead, man. If that's what he wants."

Rivera tilted his head back as Nickleson brought the bag up and poured a small portion of the contents into the man's mouth. As he began to pull the bag back, Rivera shook his head again and motioned for more. Nickleson did as he was asked and poured more of the powder from the bag until it was empty. Rivera was smiling as Nickleson lowered the bag.

"What was in that bag, Mr. Alfonso?" asked Nickleson.

"Heroin, Mr. Congressman. Enough to kill a horse," laughed the big man.

"Oh, Lord!" cried Nickleson as he turned back to Rivera. The man was smiling. His hands dropped free from his stomach. Nickleson felt a wave of nausea sweep over him as he looked down at the wound in time to see the man's intestines beginning an outward curling movement from the one-foot gash across the stomach. He jumped to his feet and stepped back as if he were afraid the organs were going to reach out and grab him. Rivera began to laugh, forcing the guts out even farther. Nickleson found that he could not take his eyes off the unbelievable sight. He watched in fascination and horror as Rivera reached down with both hands and pulled his own intestines up before his drug-crazed eyes, becoming hysterical with laughter as they slipped through his fingers. It was more than even Alfonso could stand.

The shot startled Nickleson. Rivera had taken the bullet square between the eyes; the impact blowing the back of his head out.

"Jesus!" screamed Nickleson as he lowered his hands from his still ringing ears and stared at Rivera's body, then to Alfonso and the large caliber pistol that he now lowered to his side.

"You just murdered that man," yelled Nickleson.

"That's bullshit, Congressman. The son of a bitch was killing himself. I just hurried it along for him, that's all. As far as that goes, you killed him when you poured that bag of heroin down his fucking throat."

Nickleson's hands were trembling; he had never seen a person shot before. Turning away from Rivera, he asked, "Where is Senator Kendell? Is he still alive?"

Alfonso replaced the .357 magnum in his shoulder holster and spat as he smiled, saying, "Man, you got a one-track mind, mister. Even with all this shit goin' on, you still think you gotta keep tabs on the senator. Case nobody bothered to tell ya', that's my job. An' with that fuckin' spic, Rivera, checkin' out on me, it's gonna be twice as hard."

"Is the senator all right?" asked Nickleson once more.

"Hell, yes, he's all right. You think I'd be standin' around this fuckin' jungle if he was tits up? He's just busy right now, that's all. Why don't ya go on back there and help some of them other folks? Maybe you'll get another chance to pour some of that white shit down another stupid bastard's throat," said Alfonso with a sarcastic laugh.

"What about Mr. Rivera?"

"What about him? Hell, Congressman, I know you guys can raise taxes, raise budgets, and raise hell; but I don't figure even you guys can raise the dead. The asshole's out of the game. Who gives a shit? Besides, these jungle critters gotta eat, too, ya know."

Nickleson saw no point in pushing the matter of Kendell

any farther, besides, he had to get back to Kathryn. The senator would have to join them sooner or later, anyway. Kendell's absence was but another question that would have to be added to a long, growing list of unanswered questions. Nickleson turned away from the smiling giant and walked back to the crash site. He met Howell and a small group of men as they were entering the bush.

"Edward, thank God. We heard a shot. We weren't sure what had happened. Are you all right? Where's Kendell? Karen said you went off searching for him. Is he still alive?"

"Yes, Thomas, he's still alive. I'm afraid Mr. Rivera wasn't as lucky. He was badly injured and was suffering terribly. I guess it was too much for Mr. Alfonso. He shot Rivera. That was the gunfire you heard."

"Shot him!" said someone in the group.

"My Lord," whispered Congressman Newell, Karen's husband.

"What are we going to do, now, Edward?" asked Howell.

"God, I don't know, Thomas. Has anyone checked on the pilots?"

"Yes, sir," answered one of the male staff aides. "They're all dead, sir."

"Well, that ends any chance we might have had of knowing where we are. Were the maps and charts still in the cockpit?" asked Nickleson.

"Yes, sir. I believe they were."

"Good. Get those and anything else that looks like it might give us some idea of where we are and meet us at that small clearing where the injured have been moved. Maybe we can figure something out from those maps."

"Yes, sir," replied the young aide, who turned and had only run a few steps when Nickleson called to him again, "Hey! uh—uh—"

"Percell, sir, Steven Percell."

"Thank you, Mr. Percell. While you're in there, try the radio. You know, a few of those Mayday calls that they always use. If you can't raise anyone, then write down the frequency numbers that the radio is set on. Maybe we can use them for something, depending on what paperwork we find."

Percell nodded that he understood, and tapping two of the men in the group to go along with him, the three took off for the cockpit.

"Do we have a count on how many didn't make it, Thomas?"

Howell paused a moment, the sadness in his eyes clearly showing the pain he felt. Edward had forgotten that Mrs. Howell was among the dead.

"Yes—yes, Edward. Twenty-three, counting the five-member crew. Three of the senators and their wives, Congressman Meeker, nine of the staff, Mr. Rivera, and—and my wife. There are seventeen of us left, and of that number, three of the young ladies on the staff are in critical condition. They need immediate care or I'm afraid they might die before morning. It's bad, Edward, very bad."

Howell's report cast a shadow of gloom over the small group as they made their way back to the clearing. They had all lost either loved ones or close friends in the tragedy. The thought of having to sit by helplessly and watch four more of their number die only added more misery to their already heavy burden of grief. The single hope they had for immediate assistance was the radio, but that hope vanished as Percell returned with the maps and the dreaded news that the communications system in the cockpit had been totally destroyed, as well as the frequencies the pilots may have been using before the crash. They were frightened, hurt, and totally on their own. To make matters even worse, of the twenty-one survivors, eleven were women and ten were men. A quick check of the eight in the clearing confirmed what Nickleson had feared; none of them had any military experience at all, let alone any jungle experience. Kendell and Alfonso had still not joined the group, but he doubted very seriously if either man had any more experience than they had.

Somehow, Edward Nickleson had been chosen as the leader of the group. It hadn't been said in so many words, but they were all looking at him and waiting for his instructions. It was a job he never wanted, yet someone had to do something; it would be dark soon, and so far they had done no more than count the dead and recover a few torn maps. Nickleson was no jungle expert, but he remembered what he had heard from some Vietnam veterans during his campaign. Something about the jungles burning you up during the day and freezing you at night, especially in the mountain areas. Looking around him, he realized he had no idea where they were on the maps, but one thing was clear; they were definitely in the mountains. If they were waiting for instructions, he was not going to disappoint them.

"Thomas, take Percell and three other men and collect all the cushions, blankets, pillows, and whatever else you think might serve as cover and bring it all over here. Once you have completed that, then go to the kitchen and remove everything edible. Be sure to include the sugar and salt packets, okay?"

The sudden flurry of activity was exactly what the men needed right now. It gave them a sense of accomplishing something other than just standing by helplessly.

"You've got it, Edward," smiled Howell. "Come on men, let's get to it."

Nickleson turned to the two men standing with him, "Gentlemen, we shall be the wood-gathering detail. We're going to need a lot of wood in order to keep a fire going all night. I don't want anyone going out of this clearing after dark. There's no telling what prowls around out here after the sun goes down. So, let's make sure we have plenty of wood before dark."

The two men agreed. They had just reached the edge of the clearing when Kendell and Alfonso came out of the jungle. Nickleson noticed the dirt on the senators hands.

"Have you seen my wife, Nickleson?" asked Kendell.

"Yes. She's over there near the other women. We're going out to gather wood for the night. We could use some help, Senator."

Kendell rubbed his hands and then in a matter-of-fact tone, said, "No, I don't think so, Mr. Nickleson," and

simply walked off. Alfonso grinned as he walked by
Nickleson and shook his head from side to side.

"You're a real trip, Congressman. You ain't never gonna
get no brownie points with the senator, talkin' like that. He
gives orders; he don't take 'em from nobody. You might
want to remember that."

Nickleson felt the rage building within him. He had to get
it off his chest, and this was as good a time as any.

"Fuck him and his brownie points. This isn't Washington. He doesn't have any power out here."

"You're wrong again, Congressman," smiled Alfonso as
he patted the magnum that hung in the shoulder holster.
"Matter of fact, you might say he has a hell of a lot more."

Alfonso's laugh seemed out of place among the covered
bodies and moans of pain that surrounded them, but
Nickleson knew that the man was serious about what he had
just said. The giant had already shot one man today, and
Alfonso did not seem the type that would lose any sleep
over killing one or two more. It started Nickleson thinking.
He had threatened Kendell with an investigation of his
actions on this trip; something that he was certain would not
be forgotten, even if they did get out of this alive. The
present situation offered a golden opportunity for the
senator to eliminate any chance of a problem when, and if,
they got back to Washington. Nickleson had toyed with the
idea of Kendell taking some type of threatening action but
had not seriously considered the man capable of such drastic
measures. That had been before he witnessed the ease with
which Alfonso had blown the back of Rivera's head out. He
was going to have to be extremely careful and make a point
of not going anywhere alone. One nod from Kendell and the
giant would would kill him without a second thought.
Alfonso had been right. Whether in Washington or the
middle of the jungle, Charles Kendell was a man of
power—a ruthless man, and a man to be feared.

A special hangar had been set up for Mattson and the
Rangers. Parachutes, reserves, and altimeters were lined
neatly down the center of the room. Stacks of olive drab

ammo cans were clustered by caliber along one wall next to the cases of grenades, flares, plastic explosives, claymore mines, and commo gear. Near the front of the hangar door sat the special equipment B.J. had requested. There were four long, hard-shelled gun cases, each containing a Steyr SSG Sniper rifle with infrared scopes equipped with computerized digital distance readout systems. Beside each gun case lay a black nylon bag with Velcro closures containing a silencer for the rifle. Next to the gun cases was another hard-shelled case. This one was smaller and held a total of six silencers for the fifteen-shot Beretta pistols carried by every man on the mission. Along the other wall of the hangar, resting in makeshift gun racks, was every type of automatic weapon that could be imagined. There were AR15s, Steyr AUGs, Bullpups, shotguns, machine guns, AR-16A2s, and Israeli Uzis. Parsons had not spared any outstanding favors rounding up this arsenal for Mattson and the Rangers, who stood wide-eyed like kids in a candy store, as they looked at the selection of weapons available to them. There were so many weapons that they were not sure which ones they wanted.

Mattson stepped to the center of the hangar and yelled for the rescue party to gather around him. Major Rama grabbed an ammo case and set it beside Mattson, who now stepped upon it and prepared to speak. There was perfect silence in the hangar.

"Gentlemen, we are running a little behind schedule. I had hoped to be over the target area before last light, but I'm afraid that is now going to be impossible. There is no time to send in a pathfinder team to locate and set up a drop zone for us; therefore, since it will be dark when we exit the aircraft, we will use the Salween River as our drop zone. Mr. Lassiter and I will exit first. Both of our 'chutes will have a square piece of reflective illuminating tape placed on the top center of them. Once we have opened our 'chutes, you will be able to use the tape to guide in on us. We will track for the center of the river. We will drop from fifteen thousand feet and free-fall to two thousand. Mr. Lassiter and I will fall to one thousand before opening. This will give you time to locate the tape and make any necessary adjustments for following us down."

"Now, I know you are all school qualified free-fall experts, but just the same, I have had altimeters attached to your mains; they are set to pop the 'chutes at two thousand feet. Your reserve is, of course, your manual backup, should the main fail. You'll be jumping with about seventy pounds of equipment. Your rucksacks have been fitted with self-inflating devices that activate when you hit the water, but be prepared for malfunctions.

"It is my understanding that this river can be a mother-fucker at this time of year, so if that airbag doesn't work and your equipment starts dragging you under, cut it away—let it go, and get out of the water. Don't waste time trying to recover it. We'll find you something to replace it. Is that understood?"

The hangar was silent as Mattson now looked out over the upturned faces of the young Rangers who stood stone still and quiet. They had just now begun to realize that this was all very real. It wasn't a training mission with blank adapters and blank ammunition, nor a war game scenario where they would jump in, fire a few blanks, take the objective, then go to the club for a beer; the weapons lining the walls were very real as were the bullets in the olive-drab cans. No one was going to call "time out" in this scenario.

"I said, is that fucking understood!" screamed Mattson, his loud, booming voice snapping them out of their trance and drawing from them an immediate response.

"Yes, sir!" screamed back the group.

"Very good. Now, once you have hit the water and secured your equipment, you will exit the river and begin link-up operations with those along the east bank. Should you become separated during the free-fall and land in the jungle, make your way to the river. If you are on the wrong bank, swim across. We will form up in a northerly direction. Should you find yourself too far south, continue up the east bank in a northerly direction until you link up with the rest of the unit. No one should come down to the north beyond Mr. Lassiter and me, as we will be the point;

however, should one of you overshoot us, just reverse the linkup procedure. We will remain at the rally point for approximately thirty minutes."

Mattson paused for a moment and lowered his head as he looked out over the crowd. There was a renewed serious-ness in his tone, but also a hint of sadness. "Gentlemen, if you are not at that rally point in the allotted time, you are on your own. We cannot wait, nor can we afford the luxury of sending people out to look for you. Speed is essential, and time our enemy. If you find you have exceeded the allotted time, do not bother searching for us. Turn around and immediately head south, back down the Salween River for approximately two hours; then turn due east. That will take you to the Thai border. Colonel Chakkri will alert his border patrols to be on the lookout for you. They will link you up with Colonel Decker and the Rapid Deployment Force. Now, I know that being taken back to the RDF will seem like an embarrassing experience, but let me assure you, Rangers, embarrassment is soon forgotten, but death is permanent. There are too many groups running around out there with guns for any one of you to think you can take them on single-handed, so get your asses out of there. I'd rather buy you a beer and talk about your embarrassment than hear them playing taps over you at Arlington National Cemetery. Well, that's it, Rangers. You know the rest of it. We get in, get those people, and get out. If anybody tries to stop us, we kick their asses. Do I have any questions?"

There were none.

"Okay, then, Rangers, get it on and let's go to work."

Steven Percell tossed another log on the fire and watched the embers drift skyward. The heat of the day had given way to the damp coolness of the night. Grabbing one of the light blankets from the pile recovered from the plane by Howell and his party, Percell wrapped it around himself and knelt down next to one of the four young women who had been seriously injured. The seat cushions had been used to form makeshift beds for the women. The men wished they could have done more, but given their situation, trying to make them comfortable was all they could do. The medical supplies on the plane had consisted of no more than a few aspirins, a bottle of Motrin, Band-Aids, gauze, and a couple of bottles of iodine. Hardly enough to accommodate the number of people that needed medical attention.

Nickleson saw Percell near the fire and joined him.

"How is she?" he asked.

"Pulse is dropping off. I'm afraid she's not going to make it through the night. God, I wish we could do something besides just sit here."

Nickleson knew full well the frustration the young congressional aide was feeling. The bump on Kathryn's head was apparently worse than he had first thought. She had come to for a little while and seemed to be doing better, but now she had lapsed back into a state of unconsciousness. There was no way of knowing how long that condition would last.

Nickleson looked up at the star-filled sky that peeked through openings in the jungle canopy overhead. Surely a massive search and rescue effort was already under way. It was only a matter of time before they would be found. Then Kathryn and the others could be rushed to a hospital. It had only been ten hours since the crash, but now it seemed like days.

Congressman Newell came over and knelt beside the two men by the fire.

"I would never have believed that a person could actually get cold in the middle of a jungle at night. I'm glad you had us get the stuff out of the plane, Edward; otherwise, we'd be freezing our butts off right now."

Nickleson didn't say anything; his attention was on Kendell and Alfonso. The two men were standing just out of the firelight at the edge of the jungle, Kendell was doing the talking while Alfonso was glancing over in Nickleson's direction every now and then, then back to Kendell. It gave Nickleson an uneasy feeling. Newell noticed Edward watching the two men and asked, "What's the problem between you and Senator Kendell?"

"Nothing," answered Nickleson. "You wouldn't want to

get involved in it, anyway, Thomas. It's more a personal matter, now."

Kendell had finished his conversation with the giant and returned to the area where his wife lay sleeping; he sat down beside her. Alfonso started toward the fire, then paused a moment. Reaching into his shirt pocket, he removed a small envelope, opened it, poured something into his hand, raised it to his nose and inhaled deeply.

"What's he doing, Mr. Nickleson?" asked Percell.

"If I had to guess, I'd bet he has heroin in that envelope and just took himself a hit."

"Heroin!" said Percell with excitement. "Well, hell, sir, that's nothing more than refined morphine. We can use that to ease the pain these girls are going through. Why in the hell didn't that bastard say something? We need that stuff."

"Not many people go around advertising the fact that they're carrying heroin, Mr. Percell," said Newell.

"Well, I don't care. We need that for a painkiller and he's going to have to give it up," replied Percell, as he stood up and started toward Alfonso. Nickleson jumped to his feet and tried to stop the young man, but it was too late. He was already yelling at the giant.

"Hey, you!" Alfonso looked up at the kid and smiled as he wiped some of the white powder off the end of his nose.

"Yeah. You want somethin', kid?"

Percell felt Nickleson's hand grab his arm, but he pulled free.

"Yeah, mister, we need what you've got in that envelope for the girls over there. They're suffering, and we can ease their pain with that stuff."

Alfonso's smile seemed to broaden as he held the envelope up in the firelight, laughed, and said, "Sure, kid, I'll give ya a discount. You got five thousand bucks on ya?"

"What!" yelled Percell. "Five thousand? You're nuts! Now, come on, we need that."

Nickleson looked over at Kendell for help. The senator smiled and didn't move as he sat with his back against a tree and his arms folded over his uplifted knees. He was enjoying this. Nickleson made another attempt to pull

Percell away. Percell didn't know how dangerous this man was.

"Come on, Mr. Percell, let it alone."

One of the women had regained consciousness and was crying out in agony. Percell jerked his arm free and took a step toward the giant. Alfonso folded the envelope and placed the drug in his shirt pocket, while smiling an evil grin and saying, "She don't sound too good, does she, college boy."

"You low-life son of a bitch," screamed Percell. "You give me that envelope or I'll take it."

"Come on, college boy, take it away from me."

Percell leaped forward; with his fist clenched, he swung an overhand left that the big man easily blocked and countered with a vicious blow to Percell's right jaw, sending Percell to the ground. Nickleson rushed in and caught Alfonso with a left to the side of the head, sending the big man staggering back a step. Believing he had the advantage now, Nickleson moved in closer; it was a mistake. Alfonso let him get just close enough, then he brought his foot up hard between Nickleson's legs. The blow to the groin brought a stricken moan from the congressman as he doubled over in blinding pain and fell to the ground. Others, awakened by the commotion, didn't move as they tried to figure out what was going on. Newell had leaped up from the fire when the fight had started and for a fleeting moment had thought of going to Percell's aid; but the speed with which the giant had dispatched both men caused him to hesitate. Instead, he ran to Kendell.

"Senator, you've got to stop this."

"Why? They started it. Mr. Alfonso is merely protecting himself."

The high from the heroin was beginning to take effect on the giant. He felt a sudden surge of power when he smashed Percell's jaw and an even greater high when Nickleson fell; he wanted more. Stepping forward, he waited until Nickleson was on his hands and knees, then swung his foot with all the force he could gather and kicked the man. The blow caught Nickleson in the stomach, lifting him off the ground and sending him rolling halfway to the fire. Alfonso was laughing like a madman now. Mrs. Kendell screamed to her husband, "Charles! Charles, please! Make him stop!"

Kendell pushed her away. "Shut up!"

The giant was moving in for another shot at Nickleson, who was trying desperately to get to his feet, but found that he could not get enough air. Alfonso drew his foot back once more, then he was suddenly knocked off balance when Percell hit him across the back with a two-inch-thick tree limb. The young man's choice of weapons had been a poor one. The limb broke in half after making contact with the giant's broad, muscular back. Turning on Percell, Alfonso grinned and reached for the shoulder holster. Pulling out the magnum, he cocked the hammer back while the gun hung in his hand at his side.

"You fucked up, college boy. Real bad."

Percell took a step back. His eyes widened with fear at the realization that he was about to be shot. "No, please, I—I was only thinking of the women, I—"

The thunderous roar of the magnum drowned out the boy's pleading words as the heavy slug tore a massive hole through his chest and sent him catapulting backward into the jungle. The women were screaming and the other men were afraid to move as Alfonso turned, cocked the pistol again, and took two steps toward Nickleson who still lay on the ground.

"My God, Kendell! Do something! Stop this, he's going to kill him," yelled Congressman Howell. Kendell ignored the man. Nickleson was about to get what he deserved.

Raising the gun slowly, Alfonso muttered, "So long, Congressman."

Nickleson closed his eyes and thought of Kathryn as he waited for the bullet to rip through his body. Instead of a single shot, there came a multitude of rapidly fired shots. Nickleson's eyes flew open in time to see the stunned look on Alfonso's face as he dropped the pistol and brought his bearlike hands up to the red circles that were forming on the front of his shirt. His mouth opened, but nothing came forth but a stream of blood that made its way down the side of his chin. Like a giant redwood, he fell in sections, dropping to his knees first, then onto his hands, and finally on his face, as the last breath left his body.

Everyone around the clearing sat in shock. It was as if what they had just witnessed had happened in slow motion. Nickleson pulled himself up into a sitting position and continued to stare at Alfonso's body. The women were crying, and Kendell was on his feet screaming, "Who fired those shots?"

"I did," came a voice from the jungle shadows.

All eyes turned toward the voice as armed men began to emerge from the jungle all around them with their weapons pointed at the frightened Americans. The men wore green jungle fatigues and jungle boots; a few had flop hats, but most wore rags tied around their heads like sweatbands. They were Chinese. One of the soldiers walked to the body of Alfonso. With the toe of his boot, he rolled the dead man over onto his back, fired two more rounds into his chest, then picked up the magnum and stuck it in his belt.

"Please be so kind as to raise your hands," requested the voice from the dark.

The Americans did as they were told. The soldiers swarmed around them, quickly patting them down and searching the blankets to assure that no one had any more weapons. Satisfied that there were none, the man in the darkness stepped out into the flickering edges of the firelight. He, too, was Chinese, but considerably taller and heavier than the others. He had deep, penetrating black eyes and a small pencil mustache. The khaki uniform he wore had pieces of red cloth wrapped round the epaulets of his neatly pressed shirt. He wore no hat, and his shaved head seemed to reflect the dancing flames of the fire. The round face had a look of cruelty, as if the man were feeding on the fear he saw in the eyes of the Americans.

Kendell, with his hands raised high, took a step toward the man but was abruptly halted by the bayonet on the end of one of the soldiers' rifles.

"We—we—can't thank you enough for arriving when you did. That man—that man that you shot had gone mad.

He could have killed all of us if you hadn't come to our rescue. You are obviously an officer in the army; what is your name, sir?" askcd Kendell.

The Chinese commander ignored Kendell's question as he moved to the four women that lay near death on the cushions. Turning to one of his soldiers, he said something in Chinese. The man lay his rifle down and knelt beside each of the women as he placed a finger at each one's throat to check their pulses and examine their injuries. Finished, he stood and pointed to three of the girls and shook his head from side to side as he spoke rapidly. The commander nodded, then made his way around the camp, paying particular attention to the women in the group. As he stopped and stared down at Kathryn, Edward made a move that was halted as quickly as had been Kendell's.

"Are you a search team that was sent out to locate us?" asked Nickleson anxiously, as the man knelt down and pulled back the blanket and felt Kathryn's breast through the thin blouse she was wearing.

Again there was no answer as the man stood and made a complete circle around the group, eyeing each one individually.

Kendell's arms were getting tired; he was not accustomed to being treated this way. Lowering his arms slowly to his sides, he said, "Look here, now, my name is Charles Kendell. I am a United States senator; and although I do appreciate you coming to our rescue, I must insist that you tell me when we will be getting out of here. We have been through quite an ordeal and have a number of people that are injured, as you can see. They need immediate attention."

Again, Kendell was ignored by the khaki-clad officer. Okay, he would try a different approach. Only with a little more authority this time. "Now, listen; you killed an American citizen there, mister. No matter what the reason, you still killed an American. That is not going to go well with my government; so if you want our help in explaining that, you had better start talking to me. Otherwise they're going to want to know why—"

The man spun on his boot heel and was in Kendell's face before the man could finish.

"Why? I'll tell you why, you stupid old man. Because I am General Chin Tu Ling, warlord of this province. I killed that man there not to save your miserable lives, but because he killed the younger man; and no one in my province kills anyone unless I say so. You see, Senator, I have the power of life and death here." Snapping his fingers, General Ling gave a command in Chinese, and three of his soldiers stepped forward and shot the three women, who had been pointed out earlier, through the head. Kendell's knees went weak, and he almost fell when the other women screamed. The general grabbed him by the front of his shirt and held him up.

"I know who you are, Mr. Kendell. I know who all of you are. That is why I am here. You are all my prisoners, and you will be taken to my headquarters and kept there until I can make arrangements to sell all of you to the highest bidder. Of course, the women will bring the highest price, so they will be auctioned first. Then we will see what must be done with you and these other dogs. I'm sure someone has a need for American hostages."

"You dirty basta—" screamed Nickleson, as he shoved the soldier in front of him out of the way and charged at Ling. Two soldiers fired. Nickleson's head snapped back when a bullet creased his skull, and another hit him in the shoulder driving him into the dirt. He lay perfectly still. The blood from the head wound trickled onto the jungle floor while the red on the back of his shirt spread quickly. Another soldier stepped forward and chambered a round into his rifle to put another shot into Nickleson.

"Do not waste more ammunition on the fool. Bind the prisoners; we are leaving. I want to return to my headquarters and enjoy the fruits of my labors with these American women before I sell them. Now, move!" ordered Ling.

Kendell watched as his wife was pulled to her feet. Her breast fell free from the torn blouse. One of the soldiers began to laugh. He reached out and pulled on the nipple. Wanda screamed and Ling laughed, telling the soldier to be patient; he would get his turn at the old cow before this was over. As one of the soldiers tied Kendell's wrists tightly, the senator glanced down at the body of Edward Nickleson as he thought of the suitcases that had been of so much concern to the congressman. Those suitcases were going to be Kendell's ticket out of this mess.

A soldier came over to Ling and asked about the woman who lay unconscious. Should they carry her, leave her, or shoot her? Ling walked over to Kathryn Nickleson and considered the options. Karen Newell pulled away from the soldier that had just tied her hands.

"General, please, we can carry her. She'll be all right; she just got a bump on the head; she'll be better tomorrow. Please, let us carry her."

Ling knelt down and raised the woman's skirt up her trim legs. He liked what he saw. The breasts were firm and the legs smooth. She would bring a good price, after he was through with her, of course.

"Very well, then, you and three of the women must carry her; no men. The hands of the men must remain tied; free hands give men the illusion of a chance at freedom." Ling gave the order and the ropes were removed from the four women who then placed Kathryn on a makeshift litter and carried her into the jungle.

CHAPTER 9

B. J. Mattson moved to the end of the ramp and keyed the microphone for his headset. The pilot informed him that they were twenty minutes from the river. The loud, heavy drone of the engines prevented all but shouted conversation, as he waved to Jake and relayed the time. Mortimer would be jumpmaster for Mattson's stick; then he would take his team out on his own. Adam Lassiter clumsily worked his way out of the webbed seating and haphazardly made his way to the rear of the aircraft, rucksack and weapon strapped to him. Mattson reached out and steadied the CIA man as the plane hit an air pocket and took a sudden dip.

"Jesus, I love this job, but I hate this part of the shit," yelled Lassiter.

"Supposed to build strong character, kid," replied B.J.

"Well, if pissin' in your pants every time you do this gives you character, then I'm loaded with character."

Mattson laughed as he looked down the aisles at the Rangers. Most of them sat, withdrawn, arms folded over their belly reserve 'chutes, each with his own thoughts. Some slept while others, heads back, stared up at the ceiling each man dealing with his fears in his own way. Prejump tension hung in the air like static electricity, increased even further by the knowledge that this was not just another training operation—this was for real.

Jake pressed his hands over his headset. B.J. did the

121

same; then he removed his earphones and handed them to the crew chief. The pilot had just given them the ten-minute warning. Mattson felt the plane bank, then level off on its final heading. The high-pitched whine of hydraulics set off a flurry of calm activity along the line of Rangers. They turned their heads toward the ramp and toward B. J. Mattson, who now stood at the end of the rows of seats and raised both hands palms upward, with all ten fingers spread, and yelled, "Ten minutes!"

Young eyes tried to suppress the gut-wrenching feeling that gripped every paratrooper's stomach when the count-down began. Some fiddled with chinstraps and equipment that had been checked a hundred times already, while others punched those around them to wake them up and give them the signal. Palms were rubbed back and forth on camou-flage pant legs in a futile effort to remove cold sweat from their nervous hands. At the same time, the steady whining of the hydraulics forced open the tailgate of the C-130 like some giant mouth stretching its jaws into the night to expose a black hole. A loud clank and click signaled that the hydraulics had done their job. The ramp that would lead them into the dark void beyond locked into place. Cool night air rushed in from the hole and swept down the rows of men who now stared back at Mattson; they were intently watching his every move.

Jake attached his safety line, moved out onto the wind-swept ramp, and conducted his safety checks to make sure that the ramp was locked in at the proper three degrees below horizontal. Moving back inside, he gave B.J. the thumbs-up. Mattson turned to the jumpers, placed his hands together at his stomach, brought them out to his side and back again, signaling for the Rangers to remove their seat belts. Jake placed a hand over one of the headsets again, looked to B.J., and held up six fingers. B.J. nodded, then leaned forward. Facing the jumpers, he held up six fingers and began his jump commands.

"Six minutes!"

Nervous eyes became larger.

"Get ready!"

Hands reached back and gripped the webbing.

"Port side personnel, stand up!"

The Rangers on the left struggled to their feet, the rocking, dipping aircraft fighting them all the way.

"Starboard side personnel, stand up!"

"Check equipment!"

"Sound off for equipment check!"

From the rear of the line, each man made his equipment check, then slapped the man in front of him on the rump and yelled, "Okay!" The procedure continued up the line until the first man in each line directly in front of B.J. received the slap on the butt, then stomped his foot, leaned forward, gave a thumbs-up, and yelled, "All okay!"

"Stand by!" screamed B.J. Turning to Lassiter, Mattson took him by the arm, walked him out onto the ramp, and positioned him near the very edge. He turned to the first man in his team, Lieutenant Jacoby, and waved for him to bring the men forward and line up behind Lassiter. Mattson stepped to the edge of the ramp and looked down into the blackness below. Coming up on his right, he saw the river. Its twisting, winding course reflected in the moonlight like a glittering silver scar across a carpet of black. Stepping back, B.J. winked at Lassiter and smiled as he watched the signal lights mounted near the side of the ramp. The lights' red glow cast a strange aura over the men waiting to hurl their bodies into the darkness below.

The red light winked out; it was replaced by a bright green light. Jake slapped B.J. on the butt and yelled, "Go!" Lassiter and Mattson leaped, spread-eagled, into space together. They were followed without hesitation by the rest of their team.

As the last man cleared the ramp, Jake quickly turned to Captain Ross and signaled for him to bring his team forward. The crew chief had been keeping the time and now yelled, "Thirty seconds!" Jake took his position at the edge of the ramp. The light went from red to green again, and Jake was gone, followed by Ross and the Rangers.

B.J.'s arms and legs were spread-eagled as he fell through the air. Looking over his shoulder, he saw the others strung out and suspended above him in the moon-light. He felt weightless, as the wind fluttered his cheeks and pressed against his outstretched body. Lassiter was only a short distance across from him as they fell at terminal velocity into the blackness beneath them.

Mattson forced his attention to the river, which was quickly rushing up to meet them. They were off to the left, over the trees. B.J. shifted position and planed until he was back over the center of the river.

Lassiter, following B.J.'s every move, did the same. The darkness hindered his depth perception; and even with the luminous dial, it was difficult to read the altimeter he had attached to his wrist. The 'chutes of the Rangers above them began to open as they hit two thousand feet. Lassiter would not open his chute until Mattson did.

The more B.J. descended, the faster he seemed to fall. He still couldn't get a reading off the altimeter. "Screw this! we're close enough for government work," he muttered as he pulled the main chute ripcord. He heard the fluttering of the parachute as it broke free from the backpack. The opening shock brought on by the sudden stop sent a jolt of pain into his groin and shoulders. The seventy pounds he was carrying hadn't made it feel any better. He quickly glanced upward, reassured by the square black canopy, that everything had worked like it was supposed to. He located the steering toggles and worked them until he was back on target. Quickly looking over his shoulder, he found Lassiter performing a drag action to slow down as he swung in slightly higher and directly behind him.

Mattson reached down and pulled the quick release buckles on the equipment pack. His rucksack fell away, momentarily making him feel as light as a feather. There was another jolt as the pack reached the end of the elasticized tether strap attached to his ankle. The water was coming up fast. There was a near silent pop as the rucksack hit the water. The CO_2 cartridge activated the rubber collar around the equipment and began to fill with air. On hearing the pop, B.J. reached for the main harness quick release and pulled it. His body fell free from the rig. He plunged, feetfirst, into the river and sank beneath the murky waters. Pulling the tether line free from his ankle, he surfaced and sucked in a mouthful of warm air. Treading water, he watched Lassiter splash down, then resurface and wave that he was all right. Others began to maneuver their toggles and glide softly into the water as the rangers tracked in on the point men. Except for the minimal sound of equipment and men making contact with the water, there was perfect silence. No talking. Equipment was quickly recovered, and each man quietly made his way to the east bank.

Lassiter had been first out of the water, and he now directed the first Rangers to reach the bank to take up security positions around the landing site. Pulling his equipment from the collar, B.J. scanned the moonlit sky. It was clear; everyone was down and in the water; so far, so good.

Moving along the bank, he linked up with Lassiter. Whispering, he asked, "How many have we recovered so far?"

"Counting you, me, and Lieutenant Jacoby, twenty-one."

They had exited the aircraft with a total of thirty personnel. Lady luck was still hanging with them. Only nine were missing, but they could hear people making their way along the bank. Four more Rangers came in. Twenty-five.

"Time?" asked B.J.

Lassiter lifted the cover over the face of his luminous watch.

"Eighteen minutes."

Three more Rangers joined the group. Twenty-eight. Mattson had already done better than he thought they would. Only two were missing. Master Sergeant Billy Crane, one of the few Vietnam vets with this unit, slipped quietly up next to B.J.

"Two missing, Major; Hiller and Donahue."

"Anybody know what happened to them?"

"Can't say for sure, sir. Everybody hit the water; they just haven't shown up yet."

"What were they carrying?" asked Mattson.

"Hiller had one of the SAWs; and Donahue, one of the PRC-70s."

"Damn," whispered B.J. Lady luck had extracted a price for their good fortune. B.J. had twenty-eight men, but in exchange were two of the most valuable pieces of equipment they had. The SAW was an effective base of firepower for a squad. The Squad Assault Weapon served as a light machine gun, and alone could lay down a base of fire equal to that of ten men. The loss of the PRC-70 was just as bad. Although they brought four for the mission, Mattson had learned long ago that you never have enough radios on any mission.

"B.J., you want me to go out and see if I can find them?" asked Lassiter.

Mattson considered the idea for a moment, then asked, "Time?"

"Twenty-six minutes."

"Sergeant Crane, did anyone see them go in the water?"

Crane was about to answer when Hiller suddenly appeared out of the darkness. Crane pulled him down next to them and asked, "Where the hell you been, boy?"

"Damn flotation shit didn't work. Rucksack pulled me down and got stuck in the mud on the bottom. Almost drowned my ass."

"Did you see Donahue anywhere out there?" asked Crane in a worried tone.

"Yeah, he went in a few yards from me, but I never did see him come out, Sarge."

Mattson lowered his head. He knew it had gone too easily.

"Time?"

"Thirty minutes," said Lassiter softly.

"We're out of here. Lassiter, take two men on the point with you and move out."

Crane shifted toward Mattson. The pain was in his voice.

"Major, I—I could take one man and—"

"Sorry, Sergeant. We've got to move. Maybe he got disoriented and came out on the opposite bank. If he did, he knows time's up and he'll start back south down the river. I'm sorry, Sergeant, but that's it. We're leaving."

Crane knew the major was right. All they could do was hope the kid made it out of the water and found his way back to Thailand.

"Mr. Lassiter, I'd like to be up front with you on the point if that's all right with the major," said Crane.

"I was just about to suggest that," said B.J. as he placed his hand on Crane's shoulder. "Don't worry, Sarge, the kid's a Ranger. He'll make it." Crane nodded in agreement, then he and Lassiter moved out.

Mattson stood and threw the ruck on his back. Checking the magazine in his MP-5 9mm machine gun, he turned and scanned the surface of the river one last time, hoping to see Donahue, but not really expecting to. One gone, he thought, as he headed into the jungle. He wondered how Jake and his team had made out, and if they had lost any people. B.J. had only taken a few steps when he heard what sounded like the faint echoes of thunder in the far distance. There were no clouds in the sky. The sound faded, and the night was still once again.

Jake, Captain Ross, and three of the Rangers rushed to the sound of the explosion. The charcoal-gray smoke hung heavy over the small area like a grounded cloud. Two Rangers, covered in blood, lay dead a few feet away. Another one moaned in agony from shrapnel wounds that had torn off his face. His feet kicked out wildly as his hands clutched at his face to stop the pain. The medic rushed to his side and went to work on the man.

"Oh, Jesus!" cried Ross, as he stared a short distance away at one of the trees. Halfway up, a man's waist and legs hung upside down from one of the limbs; the top half of the body was gone.

A fourth Ranger stumbled out of the brush holding his right arm. Jake ran over to him. "What the hell happened?" he asked, as he checked the wound.

In obvious pain, the young Ranger gritted his teeth and told the story. "One of the guys missed the river and got hung up. Broke his leg. We were trying to get him down. Couldn't see all that good—he slipped and the guys on the ground grabbed for him. Guess the tape had come off somehow, but—but—" The Ranger swayed slightly. He was on the verge of passing out.

"What tape? Come on Ranger, hang in there. What tape?"

"Tape on a grenade he had on his web gear. When one of the guys grabbed for him, they caught the pin and pulled it—heard the charging handle pop, then somebody yelled, and it went off— I was hit and knocked back in the brush. I—gotta sit down, sir."

Jake lowered the wounded man to the ground as the medic came over. Kneeling down to work on the man's arm, he looked up at Jake.

"That one's had it, sir. Couldn't do anything for him, shrapnel cut a main artery."

Jake turned and walked away. To be killed in combat was one thing, but losing four men because of a piece of tape had his gut twisted in a knot. Ross walked alongside him as they made their way back to the riverbank.

"We got trouble, Captain Ross," said Jake. "We jumped in here with thirty people. One broke his back in the trees; four are still missing; and now we've got four dead and one wounded—and we haven't even moved off the Goddamn river, yet." Jake Mortimer was pissed; not at Ross, nor the Rangers; but at the senseless loss of four men.

Ross was still shaken by the sight in the tree. For him the tragic accident was twice as bad; these were his men. "Any chance of getting a medevac bird in here for the boy with the broken back?" he asked.

"No way, Captain. We're too far inside Burma. Their radar would pick up a chopper coming in from Thailand in a matter of minutes. They'd scramble their Air Force and blow the thing out of the air before it could get here. The only reason we made it this far was because of the altitude we dropped from, and the C-130 flew a flight path used by the commercial airlines. No, Captain, I'm afraid the only way we're going to get that boy out of here is downriver.

We'll have to fix up a litter. We'll send the kid with the bad arm and three others back south with the litter. I hate to split us up like that, but we don't have any choice. We can't leave him here and we can't take him with us. At least this way he has a chance. What do you think?"

"Of course you're right. That'll cut us down to seventeen people. That sure isn't a hell of a lot for what we've got to do."

"I know that, Captain, but that's the way it goes. I'd like to say it'll get better, but with that grenade going off, we're really going to be in the shit. Sound travels twice the distance at night. Everybody in the neighborhood knows something is going on out here, and they'll be coming to check it out. You can count on it. Wouldn't want to get caught here with our backs to the river."

"Yes, sir," replied Ross. "I'll have the sergeant major pick the men to go back with the litter. We'll be ready to move in ten minutes."

"Fine, Captain, fine," answered Jake, as he walked off by himself. He stood by the riverbank staring down at the slowly moving water. They had lost two of the machine guns, one of the sniper rifles, and the spare ammo for the M-79 grenade launchers and 203s. More importantly, they had lost men. Weapons and ammo could be replaced by taking it from the bad guys; but men were irreplaceable out here. The Rangers had come to rescue Americans; now he couldn't help but wonder who was going to rescue the Rangers.

"Commander." Jake turned to face Sergeant Major McKinney.

"We've got the litter put together. Doc gave the boy with the broken back a hit of morphine and he gave some spare tubes to one of the guys in case they need more later. They're ready to start back. You have anything you want me to tell them?"

"No. Just make sure they know to stay with the river and keep checking their map. Hopefully they'll make it all right."

The sergeant major tried to smile as he answered, "Hell, yes, they will, sir. They're Rangers."

Mortimer watched the man walk away. Even with all the problems and only seventeen men to take on God only knows how many bad guys, he couldn't think of a better group to walk through the valley of the shadow with than these Rangers. True, there were only seventeen, but they were a determined seventeen. That made a lot of difference in this business.

Captain Ross said a few words to his men, then watched them track off to the south. Coming over to Mortimer, he said, "Commander, we're ready to move if you are. The litter crew is going to keep an eye out for the other four missing men. If they find them they'll all head back together."

Jake nodded, "That's fine, Captain. Lead the way."

Ross signaled the sergeant major, and three Rangers headed off into the jungle to take the point. Jake paused a moment to take one last look at the river. Its slowly flowing current moved endlessly along as it had done for centuries, caring little for the damage it had caused, nor for the four men in its depths, their rucksacks buried in the mud, the straps still attached to their ankles.

Marshall Parsons paced restlessly about the confines of the small operations and communications bunker of the border outpost. Jason Talbut and Colonel Chakkri were studying the terrain along the Salween River, while Lieutenant Colonel Decker and Major Rama were outside making a final check of the men and equipment of the Rangers standing by. Parsons had little experience in these matters and felt totally out of place, but it was better to be here than back at the embassy. At least here, he would be getting firsthand news of the team's progress. Mattson had wanted to limit the number of contacts and radio time until they had found the downed aircraft. Parsons now stared at the clock above the huge bank of radios along one wall. It was now 9:50 P.M.; the first scheduled radio contact was set for 2200 hours, in exactly ten minutes. Radio reports from the crew of the C-130 stated that the jump had gone perfectly, and there had been no problems going in or coming out. That news had sent an air of relief through those present. Now, if only Mattson could add to that good news by reporting that everyone was fine and the plane had been found, Parsons could pass the news to the embassy, and they, in turn, to a very anxious president and congress.

It was now 9:55. Parsons stood directly behind the radio operator, his ear finely tuned to the speaker that sat above the soldier's head. Glancing down at the CEOI of call signs taped next to one of the radios, Parsons double-checked to determine the call letters the teams would be using. Mattson was Red Rider One; Mortimer, Red Rider Two; and Decker and the outpost were Little Beaver. The one phrase Parsons hoped to hear more than any other was Little Red Riding Hood. This was the designation given to the downed aircraft. The little man pulled his watch from his watch pocket and checked it against the clock on the wall. There was less than ten seconds' difference between the two pieces.

Decker and Major Rama came in and moved to the radios. Chakkri and Talbut joined them. They all stood silently, eyes darting from the second hand on the clock to the speaker with its steady hissing sound. All they could do now was to wait.

Lassiter and Crane heard the movement at the same instant and dropped quietly to the ground. The men behind them did the same, passing the word back to Mattson that the point had contact. B.J., moving in a low crouch, made his way silently past the Rangers who now lay facing left and right, weapons at the ready. Going down on his stomach, he inched his way up to Lassiter's side and whispered, "What do we have?"

"Don't know, yet. Somebody is moving this way," came the low reply.

Mattson slowly tumbled the selector switch on his MP-5 to full automatic. Crane and Lassiter did the same. The sound drew closer. Whoever it was didn't seem to be worried about noise discipline. They were less than twenty feet from the team now and would be coming straight through the jungle and right into their lap. B.J. tightened his finger on the trigger, expecting to see either Communists or bandits coming through the brush. He suddenly let go of the trigger. What appeared was neither Communist nor bandit, but rather the head of a burro, followed by an old Burmese man with a white Ho Chi Minh beard and a stick to prod the animal along. Lassiter breathed a sigh of relief and looked to Mattson.

"Want us to grab him?" he whispered.

B.J. had started to shake his head no. However, as the burro came out into the open the moonlight highlighted something the animal was carrying on his back. That changed his mind. "Yeah, take him. No shooting."

Lassiter and Crane leaped to their feet almost directly in front of the old man, startling him half to death. Before he could cry out, Crane stepped quickly behind him and cupped his hand over the man's mouth. Mattson moved out of the shadows and walked to the burro. Strapped to the saddle were three leather suitcases and a woman's makeup case. Two of them still had the Washington, D.C. claim checks attached. Moving around the burro, B.J. stepped in front of the old man whose frightened eyes were fixed on the short machine gun in B.J.'s hands. Motioning Lassiter to his side, Mattson, still speaking in a whispered voice, said, "Tell him we are not going to hurt him. I just want to ask him some questions. Then he can go."

Lassiter nodded, then stepped closer to the old man. In fluent Burmese he relayed the message. The old man strained against Crane's grip and shook his head up and down.

"You can let him go, Sergeant, he'll cooperate with us. What do you want to know, B.J.?" asked Lassiter.

Pointing to the makeup case, B.J. said, "I want to know where he got these things from."

Questions and answers were quickly exchanged. At one point during the old man's explanation, B.J. saw Lassiter's expression take on a haunting look of concern. When the man had finished the CIA man patted his arm gently to reassure him that they had no intention of doing him harm;

then he turned to B.J., "He is from a small village only a few miles from here. They were working in the fields this morning when they saw the big metal bird pass over them. It was very low. They heard it crash in the jungle; and after much discussion among themselves, a few of the villagers went to investigate. They had intended to help if possible; but when they arrived, they saw a big man shoot an injured man in the head. They became frightened and fled back to their village. Later, the old man tried to convince the villagers to go back, but they refused. So he started back by himself. Halfway up the mountain he heard more gunshots coming from the area of the plane so he hid. Warlord soldiers came by later; they had several American men and women with them; their hands were tied. Four women were allowed to have their hands free to carry another on a litter."

"Shit!" said B.J., louder than he had intended. The outburst caused the old man to back away in fear. Lassiter raised his hand to assure him it was all right; then he looked back at B.J.

"He says there are a lot of dead people around the plane, B.J. Some killed in the crash; others have been shot."

"How many?"

"He doesn't know for sure; he just said a lot."

"How many were taken away by the soldiers?"

Lassiter asked the old man. "He doesn't know for sure, maybe ten or fifteen. He was afraid. He does have a name for us, a guy named General Ling. He says they were Ling's soldiers."

"Will he lead us back to that plane?"

Lassiter asked.

"No, sir, he doesn't want to go back up there. It is a death place, filled with evil spirits searching for the souls of the dead. He won't go back. He says it is only a mile or so from here and in the same direction we are headed."

B.J. thought about the situation for a few seconds. He could make the old man take them back, but he didn't really want to do that. They had already scared him enough. "One more question, and then he can go. Where were they taking the American prisoners?"

The old man fired off a rapid burst of Burmese and pointed to the mountains off to the right.

"He says he doesn't know exactly where, but that this guy Ling has a headquarters up in those mountains. That's where they would take them."

"Okay, I want his sacred word that if we let him go he will not say anything about seeing us out here."

The man's head bobbed up and down. A look of relief spread across his face.

"He swears on the grave of his father, and on his father's father that he will not break his word. He has seen no one," said Lassiter.

B.J. could see that this decision didn't set well with Sergeant Crane, who had drawn his knife and stood poised to cut the man's throat. B.J. shook his head no. "Okay, Lassiter, tell him he can go."

With the palms of his hands pressed tightly together, the elderly man bowed three times, and he and his burro wandered off into the darkness as B.J. checked the time. It was ten after ten. He was late with his situation report to Decker.

"Sergeant Crane, have the commo man set up for contact with Little Beaver. They're probably going through a nut roll because we're ten minutes over our contact time." Crane left. "Lassiter, I want you to take Lieutenant Jacoby and half the men, locate that plane, and set up a perimeter around the thing. We won't be more than fifteen minutes behind you. If you run into some shit, come up on the team push and give your situation. We'll just have to play it by ear from here on out. Any questions?"

"No, sir."

"Well, let's hit it then. Looks like it's party time." said B.J. as the two men went back to the team.

Jacoby and Lassiter were gone by the time B.J. had established contact with the outpost. Parsons was extremely upset that they were fifteen minutes late with their report. Mattson took the verbal abuse from the little man with a grain of salt because he was right. They were late. Having released his pent-up frustrations, Parson finally let B.J. give him his report. The bad news was the loss or disappearance of Donahue, the good news was that they had a positive fix on the crash and were moving to secure the area. There were known fatalities, but he could give no names at the moment. Relaying the information about the warlord Ling and the prisoners brought a flurry of questions from Parsons and Decker, most of which he couldn't answer. Colonel Chakkri was familiar with General Ling and warned B.J. that the man was totally ruthless, could not be trusted, and would not hesitate to kill all of the Americans he now held. Decker informed B.J. that Generals Johnson and Sweet would arrive at the outpost before noon the next day. B.J. scheduled another contact for zero one hundred hours. The team should be at the crash site and have a body count, plus some names for them by then. Parsons reminded Mattson that 1:00 A.M. meant just that, 1:00 A.M. Mattson assured the little man that they would be on time and asked if he had had any contact with Red Rider Two. Parsons told him no, then added rather sarcastically that punctuality was neither man's strong point. B.J. took the remark in stride and signed off.

Once the radio gear was stored away and they were ready to move again, B.J. joined Sergeant Crane on the point. They moved off in the direction of the plane. He had thought of calling Jake to let him know they had a fix on the aircraft, but he thought it best to wait until it could be confirmed. It wouldn't be the first time B.J. had been lied to by a little old man. It had happened all the time in Vietnam. But then, if this were still Vietnam he wouldn't have stopped Crane from using his knife.

They had covered over half a mile when Lassiter came up on the squad radio. They had found the plane. The old man had not lied; there were dead people everywhere. The initial count was twenty-seven, and they were still searching. Lassiter paused a moment, then came back with, "We've got a live one. Say again, we have found a live one. He has been shot a couple of times but he is alive. Doc says he'll make it. Do you copy, Red Leader? Over."

"Roger, we're coming in. Try to retrieve as much

identification as possible on the dead and alert Red Rider
Two that we have found the plane. Give him a coordinate
and tell him to link up with us at that spot. Copy, over?"

"Roger, copy, Red Leader, out."

The fact that Jake and Captain Ross had not made contact
with Decker and the outpost had Mattson worried. Hopefully, by the time they reached the plane Lassiter would
have talked to Jake and would know their situation. That
thought was on his mind when Crane suddenly stopped and
stood stone still. B.J. automatically did the same. The men
behind them stopped, knelt down, and took up the slack in
their triggers. B.J. tried to spot what had caused the action
by the sergeant. Out of the corner of his eye, he saw Crane
staring to his left front along the edge of the jungle. B.J.
focused his eyes on the spot, straining to see something that
shouldn't be there. Then he saw it—a rifle barrel. It was
barely visible; only a few inches highlighted against the
contrasting greens and browns of the jungle.

"Ambush," whispered Crane as he thumbed the selector
switch on his rifle to full automatic. The very word sent a
chill all the way up B.J.'s back. They had walked right into
it, but how far? Mattson counted at least five more barrels
beyond the first one he had spotted. Slowly moving his head
to the left, he spied three more directly to their left and a
little behind them. He didn't know how far they were into
this thing, but it really wasn't going to matter; he and
Sergeant Crane were as good as dead already. He could tell
that Crane knew that, too.

"American!" came a voice from the shadows. "I think
we got you pretty good. Yes, I do. Be so kind as to lay your
weapons down and tell your men to do the same, please. I
have no desire to waste ammunition nor to see you killed."

Crane glanced over at B.J. "They got us cold turkey,
Major; but it's your call."

"Shit," thought B.J. to himself. Crane was right. They'd
be lucky to get off one magazine before they would be torn
apart by the ambush.

"Please, American," came the voice again. "You have
only fourteen men, while I have forty that are pointing their

guns at you right now. Your friends at the airplane are surrounded, too; they just don't know that yet. Your actions will kill not only you, but them as well, so, please, lay down your guns and we can talk, okay?" The voice did not sound threatening in any way.

"You figure he's got that many, Major?" asked Crane.

"I'd like to say, no, but I couldn't feel any more eyes staring at me if I were wearing Dolly Parton's chest. We got no choice, Sergeant, put 'em down." Turning to the men behind him, B.J. yelled, "Put your weapons on the ground and stand with your hands up. Don't anyone fire. That's an order." Mattson felt naked standing without his rifle and his hands raised.

The man in the shadows had lied. He didn't have forty men; the number was closer to sixty. They wore a mixed match of uniforms, fatigue shirts, blue jeans, camouflage pants, and a variety of colored shirts. Some had jungle boots, others wore tennis shoes. Their weapons were as mixed as their clothes; everything from Russian AKs to an old .45 caliber grease gun. "Bandits," whispered B.J.

"Oh, that is very smart move on your part, American. I no like having to shoot people before we have chance to talk. Sometimes can make big mistake and shoot wrong person. You know, how they say, fuck up."

B.J. and Crane turned to face the man who had stepped from the trees. He stood no more than five-feet-three and had to weigh at least 230 or 240 pounds. He had the only complete uniform in the group: camouflaged jungles with jungle boots and a pistol belt that strained its every link to contain the robust gut that extended a good two feet out over the toes of his boots. His face was full and round with small ears that stuck out from a nearly bald head which sprouted a single mass of hair wrapped in a pigtail along the right side. When he smiled, two gold teeth glittered in the moonlight. Eyebrows were practically nonexistent above the slightly slanted, playful black eyes. As the Rangers were being rounded up and herded into a tight circle around B.J. and Crane, the man bent down and picked up Mattson's MP-5, admiring the smoothness of the weapon.

"Oh, yes, this is very fine equipment. If only I could have such guns as this for my men." Looking up at Mattson who stood six-four, the man flashed the golden teeth and reached to shake B.J.'s hand as he said, "I am Aung Y' San and these are my men. I would think you are here to the airplane of the the—the, big wiggens? Is that how you say that?"

"Bigwigs," replied Mattson.

"Ah, yes, bigwigs. My English, it pretty good, but some of your sayings I find verrrry difi—dific—very hard. And your name?"

"Mattson, B. J. Mattson."

"I would think you to be a colonel; is that correct?"

"Close, Mr. San, I am a major."

"Oh, I not a mister, I am a general. Everyone who have a army in Burma, be it little army or big army, they are general."

"Okay, General, so what side are you on—Communist, Burmese, Karan, Shan, what?"

San's belly actually rolled when he laughed. Releasing B.J.'s hand after a firm grip, he rolled his little eyes as he answered, "Oh, noooo, Major B.J., my men and I fight for the Aung Y' San Movement of Burma. They fight for me, I fight for them. We fight everybody—Communist, Burmese, anybody that want to fight; we good at that. At first we thought you were Burmese patrol. See chance to maybe have a little fun, but you too big to be Burmese, so thought better we talk first."

"Bandits," said B.J.

"Yessss, just like your country, America have famous bandits, I famous Burma bandit, much like your Jesup James."

B.J. couldn't help but smile as he said, "Jesse James."

"Yes, him, too," grinned San. "Tell me, Major. You come for your big—wigs, no?"

"Yes, but we have been told that the survivors were taken away by soldiers."

"Burmese soldiers?" asked San.

"No, the soldiers of a warlord named Ling."

The smile dropped from San's face like a lead weight. The playful eyes suddenly went dark as a frown replaced the smile.

"That is very, very bad. I had hoped to get here with my men before anyone else. Villager came to my camp, told of plane carrying Americans falling from the sky. I think maybe your America pay San very much money for saving lives of hurt Americans but now—is very bad, Major. This man Ling is bastard from long time back; he very cruel and powerful man. I think maybe you don't see your hurt Americans no more, and San no make money for his army. Is too bad."

Mattson's mind was racing now. San obviously had a great dislike for General Ling, something that B.J. could put to good use if he played his cards right. "Listen, General San, maybe we can help each other. You need money and I have a mission to save those Americans. How many men do you have?"

San might be a short, fat man, but he was nobody's fool. He knew where B.J. was going with that question. "Three, maybe four hundred, I not sure. Some go home to plant crops this time of year; others just to find a woman for a few days. I run a very relaxed army, Major. When my army wants to fight, they come back; when they don't, they don't."

"Do you know where Ling's headquarters are and how many men he has?"

"Of course, Major. I would be a very sorry general were I not to know such things. He has a fortress less than five miles from here in the mountains. I would guess his strength to be perhaps six to seven hundred men." Lifting Mattson's rifle in his chubby hand, he said, "And they have fine weapons like these. Ling does not have to rob and steal as we do. He makes a fortune from the poppy fields in this area. He deals very heavy in the drug market and lives like a king at his fortress. I have done battle with him only once, and it turned out very bad for me and my army; his weapons were better than ours. I lost many men that day, Major. It is a poor general that will send his men into battle with weapons as ancient as the ones we carry. As you can see, many are from the time of the great war, when we fought the Japanese. My grandfather often talked of how the Americans helped us during those days. That is why, when I saw you were American, I did not kill you and your men. However, I sense that you are about to make me an offer, Major. My men for money or weapons. Is that not right?"

"Something like that, General San. I believe my government would be most grateful to anyone who assisted me in the rescue of our people."

"Ah, so, I help you and you promise that your government will be grateful; is that right?"

"Yes. I can promise you will get something for your trouble," answered Mattson.

"I mean no disrespect, Major, but did your government not promise to help the Indians of your own country? Then of course there were your promises to the Koreans, the Vietnamese, and certain countries of Africa and Central America. I am afraid your country's record of keeping its promises has reached even those of us in these remote parts of the world, Major. The lives of my men today for the promises of your government tomorrow hardly seems, how you say, a square deal." San paused and studied the disappointment he saw in Mattson's face. The American knew that without his help, he had no chance of rescuing the survivors. Admiring the workmanship of the MP-5 one last time, he reached out the hand holding the weapon and passed it back to Mattson, then instructed his soldiers to return the Rangers' weapons.

"Major, you and your men may keep your weapons. Now come, we will go the short distance to where the plane crashed. I think much better when I am walking; it will give me time to consider your offer. Although, I must warn you, I promise nothing. I suggest that you call your men and tell them we are coming. Jungle darkness and moving sounds in the night have a tendency to cause nervousness in those not accustomed to such things. I would not like to be the one shot by mistake."

Mattson agreed and nodded to Crane to make the call. "I

hope you consider my offer, General. Either way, I still have a job to do. We will get those people back or die trying."

"Ah, my newfound friend, it is easy to see why they send such a man for this dirty business. I see fire in your eyes and hear determination in your words. Yet those things do little to change the odds which you and your brave men shall have to face at Ling's fortress. Still, one can never tell which way the gods may choose to smile upon mortal men. I like you, Major. You, like I, have a warrior's heart." San rubbed his chin for a moment and looked Mattson up and down, then laughed, "If only I had such a stomach to go with that heart."

Crane stepped up to B.J. "Sir, I told Mr. Lassiter that we were coming in with some people and not to fire them up. He wanted you to know that the the guy they found is a congressman named Nickleson. Says the guy has quite a story to tell and wants us to link up, ASAP."

"What about Jake?" asked B.J.

Sadness gripped Crane's voice as he replied, "Not good, sir. He lost ten people on the river. Lassiter gave him the location of the plane. They're moving to link up with us now. Jake said he'd tell you about it when he sees you at the crash site."

San saw the pained expression come over Mattson when he heard that ten men had been lost. His numbers were dwindling. The thought of attacking the fortress was becoming more and more like a madman's dream.

"General, if you'll lead the way, I'd like to head for the crash site," said B.J.

San shouted orders to his men, and three of the bandits moved to take the point with General San, B.J., and the Rangers following close behind.

CHAPTER 10

General Ling ripped a leg from one of several roasted chickens on the platter in front of him. He was fully aware that the hungry eyes of his prisoners were watching his every move as they stood bound and lined up before the table. He did not know the last time they had eaten, nor did he care. Wiping his mouth with the back of his hand, he continued to chew as he looked at the six women and seven men who were now his to do with as he pleased. He had had the woman on the litter taken to his room where his personal physician was presently examining her and caring for her injuries. He now waited for the doctor to give him the results of the examination, for it was well after midnight and he planned to retire soon. If the woman's condition was not improved, he would have to choose another to spend the night in his bed. The woman they had called Kathryn was the best of the group, but if she had not improved, she would be of no use to him. There was no challenge to raping an unconscious woman. She would lie there, and he had enough of that from the local village girls already. No, it had to be a woman who would fight him, kick and claw, bite and scratch; a woman he could slap into submission. Amid her screams and crying, he would ravish her body in every way imaginable until he controlled her very soul. His eyes scanned the choices before him and came to rest on Karen Newell. Her proud face, long hair, and uplifted breasts promised firmness which stirred arousal between his legs. She would be his choice.

"Now, look here General Ling, I think you fail to realize the mistake you are making by holding us here against our will. The Unites States government will not permit such blatant disregard for the proper treatment of its political leaders and fellow Americans. Now, if I were you, I'd—"

Ling threw the remains of the chicken leg at Kendell, hitting the man in the chest with the bone and leaving a grease stain on the senator's shirt.

"You will keep your mouth shut!" screamed Ling as he jumped to his feet and pointed a finger at Kendell. "You will not speak unless spoken to. It is you who fails to recognize you situation, old man. It is you who has made the mistakes, not I. You, and men like you, are the ones who have placed Burma in such turmoil. It was you who cut off aid to this country and its new military leaders. Do you honestly think that they will come here to save those who voted to take money from them? You are a fool if you believe that, Mr. Kendell. But then, that is not a rarity in Washington, is it?"

Kendell stood, humbled and frightened, before the warlord, not knowing if and how he should answer the man's slander of his high office and of his government. It was Wanda Kendell who came to her husband's aid as she stepped forward, pointed her finger at Ling, and cried, "You will regret this one day, you overbearing, conceited, cheap excuse for Fu Manchu! You'll long regret this day."

Kendell and the other prisoners stared at the chubby woman in shocked amazement. Ling himself was stunned by the outburst and now stood speechless, with his mouth open. Had it not been for the sudden laughter of some of Ling's officers, she might have gotten away with it. But now Ling had been embarrassed in front of his men. He had to do something to save face, and quickly. A cruel smile etched its way across his face as Ling joined in the laughter and sat back down in his gold plated chair with red velvet cushions.

"Senator Kendell, is this cow your wife? I would think a

man of your power and influence would prefer to spread his seed among younger and more shapely whores like those around you now."

"You bastard!" shouted Wanda Kendell.

"Wanda! Please, shut up," said Kendell. "We're in enough trouble as it is without you shooting off your mouth."

"I will not shut up! Someone has to stand up to this animal."

Ling laughed as he said something to his officers, and they, too, began laughing. Looking up at Kendell, Ling said, "I told my officers this cow has more balls than all of you men put together. Wouldn't you agree, Mr. Kendell?"

"If you say so, General Ling."

Wanda was about to tear into Ling again when the doctor came into the room, walked up to the general and whispered something in his ear. Ling frowned, then nodded for the man to leave. Ling stood and walked around the table to where Karen Newell stood, her husband's hands gripped tightly in her own. The evil grin on Ling's face sent a shiver through her. She could see the wanton lust in his eyes as he leaned closed to her face and said, "Your friend is going to be all right, pretty one. She needs only to rest a while. My doctor says she will be better by tomorrow. Is that not good news?"

Karen moved closer to her husband as Ling gently stroked the length of her arm. She could smell the chicken still fresh on his breath as he raised the hand higher and began stroking her long, brown hair.

"Such kindness on my part should be rewarded, don't you think?"

Karen's voice was caught in her throat. She was terrified of this man.

"Now, that's enough," said Thomas Newell. "We are grateful that you have helped Mrs. Nickleson, but that doesn't give you the right to paw my wife. I would appreciate it if you would please take your hands off her."

"Or what, Mr. Newell? Are you going to threaten me?" smiled Ling as he allowed his hand to drop lower along

Karen's shoulder to the smooth skin above V neck of her blouse.

"You son of a bitch!" screamed Newell as he pulled his tightly bound hands from Karen's. He tried to swing at Ling, who laughingly stepped aside, showing remarkable speed as he leaped up and kicked his foot straight out and into Newell's midsection. The vicious blow doubled the man over and sent him onto the marble floor, grasping for air. Karen fell to his side and cradled his sagging head in her arms as she looked up at Ling and begged him to stop. Ling only laughed and yelled to one of his soldiers to pull the woman out of the way. Rough hands jerked her to her feet and dragged Karen to the front of the table. She watched in horror as Ling reached down, gripping a handful of her husband's hair, and pulled him up onto his knees. He swayed for a moment; his breathing was still labored and his eyes confused, uncertain of where he was. Releasing Newell's hair, Ling pivoted on his left foot and swung his right foot waist high in a half circle with full force. The heel of his right boot struck Newell in the back of his head and sent him pitching forward. His nose cracked as it made contact with the marble floor. Blood went everywhere. The women began to scream. Congressman Howell and two of the male aides made an attempt to step between Ling and Newell; their efforts brought on a flurry of open-handed blows to their faces and midsections from Ling's officers, driving them to their knees.

The women were crying; Karen was screaming for Ling to stop. She would do anything he wanted if only he would stop.

The sight of Newell's blood running out into the marble floor had sent Ling's officers into a frenzy—like a pack of sharks sensing blood in the water. Now all of the men were being attacked, punched, slapped, and beaten to the floor. Kendell was begging for mercy as he tried to crawl away from the never-ending hail of blows that rained down on him. Karen was hysterical as she desperately tried to reach her bleeding husband's side. Ling was laughing, like the mad ringmaster he was at this circus of horrors that surrounded him.

Then it started. The inevitable act that had been slightly building from the very beginning. The officers held back only until their leader made the first move. Ling kicked Newell in the side of the head like one would kick a football, then stomped the heel of his boot firmly down onto the neck of the fallen congressman, breaking his neck. The awful sound of the spine snapping brought a halt to the beating of the others, as the officers watched Newell's body arch upward at the midsection; an action brought on by the severed nerves of the spinal column and the involuntary final reactions of a dead man.

Ling stepped back to survey his handiwork. The room was silent except for the weeping and crying of the women. The officers waited with anticipation for what they knew would come next. Ling did not disappoint them. Karen stared down at her dead husband; she was in a state of shock as Ling grabbed her arm with one hand, and with the other, tore her blouse and bra from her body. The officers all cheered and descended on the women like a pack of wild dogs, ripping and tearing the clothes from the screaming women, who were now thrown to the floor, or onto the table amid the food, and raped repeatedly by one officer after the other.

Kendell raised his bloody and battered face to see his wife on the floor, naked, with one man on top of her and three others standing to the side laughing as they cheered their comrade on. Ling had Karen Newell on the table, slapping her as he tore the last of her clothing from her body. She was crying, begging him to stop, but the man heard nothing. Dropping his pants, he climbed upon the table between her legs. Hooking his hands behind her knees, he jerked her legs up and pulled her toward him. Her screams increased. Ling reached down onto the table and grabbed an apple; he shoved it into Karen's mouth, silencing her pleas for mercy. Laughing sadistically, Ling pushed himself into her and grunted wildly with each brutal thrust of his body, squeezing and clawing at her bare breast.

Everywhere women screamed and cried among the cheering, laughing, sweating men who breathed heavily around them and on top of them. It was a nightmare come true. A nightmare that now slowly began to fade before Charles Kendell as he lost consciousness.

It was nearly dawn when Jake Mortimer and Captain Ross arrived at the crash site with Red Rider Two. Both men were as surprised to see the number of people at the site as Lassiter had been when B.J. had shown up with San and his bandits. Mattson made the introduction. Lassiter commented that he had heard of the famous Burma bandit. San grinned, showing his two gold teeth and threw his shoulders back and his chest out. He quickly told his bandits what Lassiter had said, placing special emphasis on the word, famous. From that moment on the young CIA man could do no wrong in General San's eyes.

Jake sadly explained the incident at the river. It was unfortunate, but what was done was done. B.J. and Jake now went to the area the medics had set up to care for Congressman Nickleson. The shot to the head had been a near miss, and the wound to the shoulder had been a clean shot that had proven more painful than deadly. Nickleson had told an interesting story to Lassiter when they found him. He repeated the same story to B.J., who went over the details with Jake and Captain Ross.

"So what does all this mean?" asked Ross, after B.J. had finished.

"Damn if know, Captain. We checked out those guys, Rivera and Alfonso. They're definitely not Secret Service or company men. They look more like mob guys to me," replied B.J.

"You gotta be kidding, B.J. What the hell would a senior senator be traveling with mob guys for?"

"Hey, like I said, Captain, that's just my opinion. I have no more idea of what's going on than you do. I just find it strange that a senator would stand by and let his bodyguard blow away a congressional aide, then watch while the same guy beat a congressman half to death without saying a damn thing. It doesn't make any sense."

"You sure this Nickleson guy isn't just confused?" asked Lieutenant Jacoby.

"He's not confused, Lieutenant. One look at the guy and you can tell somebody beat the shit out of him, and there is no doubt that he was shot. So you tell me what the hell is going on out here," said B.J.

"What about the mysterious suitcases?" asked Jake.

"Nickleson said he saw dirt on the senator's hands after Alfonso blew away his partner. He figures Kendell buried the bags somewhere in the jungle beyond the tail section which is about a hundred feet behind us. I've got Lassiter and a squad checking the area out to see if they can find anything. But for right now, we've got bigger problems than a couple of suitcases. General San tells me that this character, General Ling, has close to nine hundred men working for him, and that fortress of his is built like Fort Knox. They've got our people in there, and we have to figure a way to get them out."

"B.J., there's no way we can pull it off with just our people. We're going to need some help. Has San decided what he's going to do yet?" asked Jake.

Doubt registered in B.J.'s eyes as he replied, "No, not yet, but I wouldn't count on him doing any more than showing us where this fortress is. He's a likable little shit, but he's a businessman and a leader, too. I can see his point; this isn't his problem. Why should he get a bunch of his people killed for nothing but promises from a country that hardly ever keeps its word about anything."

"Good point," said Jake, who then laughed. "Shit, here I am, a Navy commander with a couple of million family dollars in a bank in Philadelphia, and I bet this guy wouldn't take a check. Now ain't that a bitch!"

The four officers were laughing as Adam Lassiter pushed his way through the brush and stepped into the clearing. He carried a brown leather suitcase in each hand, and there was a huge smile on his boyish face.

"Hey, fellows, you'll never guess what I have here."

B.J. and the others stopped laughing and walked over to Lassiter.

"Well, I'll be damned. Where did you find them?"

"Just like Nickleson said, they were buried about thirty yards back from the tail section; and, brother, you ain't gonna believe what's in here."

"Well open'em up," said Ross; his voice filled with excitement.

"You think they're ready for this, Sergeant Major?" said Lassiter as he winked at McKinney and tossed the bags on the ground.

"I really doubt it, Mr. Lassiter," replied the sergeant major as he knelt down next to one of the bags and flipped the locks while Lassiter did the same to the other bag. General San and a few of his officers walked up to the small group and watched with the same baited interest as the others as the suitcases were opened.

"Holy mother of Buddha!" exclaimed San, his eyes as big as silver dollars.

Lassiter watched the expressions on the faces of the officers around him, each showing the surprise and shock in a different way. Captain Ross knelt down and ran his fingers lightly over the top row. "Is it real?" he asked.

"As far as I can tell, it is, sir," answered Lassiter.

B.J. turned to General San, who was still in a trance, his black eyes seeing nothing but the bright green of the money that filled his both suitcases to the very top. "Well, General, looks like we're out of the promising business. How about us paying U.S. currency for the use of your army for one day?"

San was at a loss for words. He had never imagined there could be that much money in the world.

"How much is in there, Lassiter?" asked Jake.

"Best the sergeant master and I can figure, somewhere around two million dollars."

That remark brought a low whistle from some members of the group, and even sent San back a few steps. Cursing, he slapped the side of his head as he said, "This money

could have been ours, had we only found the plane first.
Buddha surely does play a cruel joke on San."

"I don't know who that money belonged to before this,
General, but it's ours now. Being an authorized agent of the
U.S. government involved in a crisis situation, I figure I
have the power to do what I feel is necessary to save the
lives of American citizens. Those suitcases are yours if you
will help us," said B.J. Mattson.

San was still in awe of the total amount of money
involved. "You do not jest, Major B.J. You mean what you
say?"

"Absolutely, General. A fact, not a promise. You help
us, and that money is yours to do whatever you want."

San quickly stepped forward, clasped Mattson's hand
tightly, and began to pump it up and down as he shouted
orders to his officers, who saluted smartly, and took off at
a dead run in all directions.

"You have a deal, Major B.J. I send my men to gather
my army; they will bring them here to this place. It will take
three or four hours, but that will give us time to make a
plan. I think it wise that we take a small group to the fortress
so you may see the task that lies before you."

Pulling his hand free from the iron grip of the grateful
man, B.J. agreed and told Ross to form up a recon patrol.
San, Lassiter, and he would be going with them; Jake and
the others would remain with Nickleson and the plane. The
site was now alive with activity as the men checked
weapons and equipment and prepared to leave. Jake walked
with B.J. as he went to tell Nickleson of the suitcases and
their contents.

"That money answer any questions for you?" asked Jake
as they walked.

"I've been adding it up, and it comes out bad every
time," replied B.J.

"Me, too. I get the feeling our Senator Kendell had a
little job on the side, a pretty profitable one at that. At least
it answers my questions about those two gorillas that were
with him, and why they weren't worried about carrying
heroin around with them. Just happens to be the drug of

choice in these parts, and two million will buy a hell of a lot of the stuff."

"Yeah, at least Nickleson will know he was right about those bags," said B.J.

"I don't think the guy cares about that anymore. He's more worried about his wife and those other people right now."

"From what San says, he has good reason to be worried. I just hope we're not too late." As they neared the area where Nickleson was lying, B.J. whispered, "Jake, try and make this operation sound like a walk around the park. The news about the money should give him a lift. No need in following that with the truth about how hard this is going to be, okay?"

"I agree," said Jake, "and in a way you're right, you know. It's us walking through Central Park with a couple of million bucks and a big sign that reads, 'Mug Us!' and brother, this park is full of muggers that would like our head on a stick."

"That reminds me, don't let me forget to call back to Little Beaver and tell them the plan. General Johnson should be at that location just about the time we're ready to go with this thing."

"Yeah, but so will our boy Sweet," said Jake dryly.

"I know, that remark about a head on a stick is what reminded me." grinned B.J.

Kathryn Nickleson slowly opened her eyes and found herself staring up at the flowing golden cloth that formed a canopy above the bed where she lay. Her head still bothered her and the muscles in her neck and back felt stiff as she sat up and looked around the room, trying to figure out where she was. Judging by the light from the window, it was early morning. Her first instinct was that they had been rescued, and Edward had spared no expense to see to her comfort and care. But where were they? It had to be Thailand. There were carvings of elephants and Buddha mixed with bright colors of cloth in shimmering gold, red, and blue. But where was Edward?

Slipping out of the bed, she looked for a robe, but there was none. Her torn and tattered clothes from the crash lay piled next to the bed. The only thing she now wore was her bra and panties. Searching around the room for something to wear, she spotted what appeared to be a closet. Opening the sliding bamboo doors, she was surprised to find rows and rows of military uniforms in a variety of colors each with a multitude of ribbons and medals of all shapes and sizes hanging from them. At the end of one row she spied what she was looking for, a bright red robe of pure silk with a golden dragon embroidered on the back. It was beautiful. Kathryn didn't know who this all belonged to, but whoever it was surely wouldn't mind if she wore the robe. After all, she was a guest in their home.

Tying the robe securely at the waist, she ventured to the door and stepped out into the hallway. She found a long, extravagantly decorated corridor that ended in a spiral staircase leading downstairs. Due to the early hour, she began to feel as if she were the only one in the place up and moving around. But where was Edward? Where was anybody? Reaching the end of the corridor, she placed her hand on the railing and began to descend the staircase. Her mind was ill-prepared for the sight that greeted her as she neared the bottom of the stairs. Her hands went up to her face as she gasped and whispered, "Oh, my God!"

There on the floor before her lay the battered and crumpled naked bodies of Mrs. Kendell and four of the staff aides from the plane. No less than twenty naked oriental men lay around them. Boots and uniforms were scattered about the large room amid empty whiskey and wine bottles. Her eyes darted about the room for some sign of Edward or Senator Kendell, but they were not there. The only man with any clothes on lay in an awkward position in the very center of the room.

Kathryn forced herself to walk the remainder of the way down the stairs and onto the cool marble floor. Her mind was reeling, trying desperately to make some sense of the scene around her. Each step brought her closer to the man lying in the center of the room; there was something red, almost rust colored spread on the floor around the man's head. It was not until she was only a few feet away that she realized that the rust color was blood and the man was Karen Newell's husband. His bloody, swollen, and discolored face was barely recognizable.

Bringing her hand up to her mouth, Kathryn struggled to stifle a scream. Fear gripped her soul as she backed away from the terrible sight. A low moan from somewhere on her left startled her. She jerked her head around and saw Karen Newell slowly dragging her nude and battered body from under the huge table near the wall. Kathryn raced to her friend's aid. Kneeling, she took Karen's head in her arms and lowered it to her lap. Karen's face was swollen. A small trickle of dried blood stained the side of her mouth and nose. There were ugly scratches and red marks on her breast and dark black bruises along the insides of her thighs. Reaching up onto the table, Kathryn removed a glass that contained water. Wetting the end of the silk robe, she dabbed at the bloody spots and gently wiped Karen's face and forehead. Tears began to form in her own eyes. What in the name of God had happened here? Where were the men? Poor Robert Newell!

The water began to bring Karen around. Slowly, cautiously, she tried to open her eyes, but she could only manage to open the right one; the left one was swollen shut from the beating she had taken from Ling. Seeing Kathryn, she reached out for her friend's hand and gripped it tightly. Her first attempt at trying to talk sent a river of pain through her face and a moan from her lips.

"It's all right, Karen. Don't try to talk right now. I'll get some help."

Karen tightened her grip on Kathryn's hand and shook her head from side to side. "No—no, Kathryn. Run away—get out of here while you—while you can— Robert—is dead, they killed him—they raped us—you must get away. Hurry. Leave me and—run, Kathryn, run— away."

"Karen, who did this? Where is Edward? How did we get here?"

"Get away—Kathryn. Don't let Ling find you—Edward is dead, Kathryn, just like my Robert. You have to run! Go Kathryn, go now."

Edward, dead? No, that had to be a mistake. Karen didn't know what she was saying. He couldn't be dead, he just couldn't. "Karen, where are the men? Senator Kendell and the others?"

Karen was finding it easier to talk now. She tried to raise herself up and out of Kathryn's lap, but found the pain from her bruised abdomen too painful.

"They beat them before the raping started. I saw them drag Congressman Howell and three of the staff away by their feet, while—while—" her voice caught for a moment before she continued, "while Ling was raping me. Senator Kendell was unconscious, I believe. For some reason they left him where he was. Later, when Ling had finished with me another—another man took his place. I saw Kendell on his knees begging Ling to listen to him. I don't know what they said. I couldn't hear. There were—were other men doing things to—to me." Karen broke down and began to weep. "Oh, Kathryn, it was so awful; they did terrible things to me—and the others. Poor Wanda, I can still hear her screaming; I don't even know if she's still alive. They were especially hard on her. She dishonored General Ling by talking back to him. They—were taking turns with her and—and sticking things in her. I couldn't watch anymore; I closed my eyes and hoped I would die."

Kathryn held her tightly in her arms and rocked her as if she were a baby. "I know, I know, Karen, but it's over now. You are alive, Karen, that's all that matters." Kathryn continued to hold her tight, wanting to ask again about Edward but certain in her own mind that the poor woman was in shock and didn't realize what she had said. There was no way Edward could be dead. She could feel it, much as she had sensed that the plane was going to crash. No, Edward was not dead; she had to believe that. But what was she to do now? She couldn't leave Karen, Wanda, and the others, but what should she do? What could she do?

"Ah, the sleeping beauty has risen."

The words seemed to come from nowhere, causing Kathryn to turn quickly to look behind her. General Ling stood over her, staring down at her frightened expression. He asked, "How do you like the robe? It is one of my favorites."

Kathryn tried to comprehend how the man could be so casual amid the carnage that lay all around him. "Are you the man in charge here?" she asked, trying to shield the fear she felt deep in her stomach.

"You might say that," laughed Ling as he bowed at the waist, "General Chin Tu Ling, at your service, madam."

"Then you are the one responsible for this," said Kathryn, nodding her head toward Karen, who had closed her eyes and begun to shake at hearing the man's voice.

Raising his hands playfully and maintaining a conceited grin on his face, he replied, "I cannot admit to the scratches on the breasts, but as to providing this whore with the ultimate sexual experience of her obviously miserable life, then yes, I am guilty. Had I not consumed more than my share of your American whiskey and sampled the favors of this one, as well as the favors of the other five during the long night; you too would have experienced such wonders as your friends did.

"But, unfortunately, I was overcome by fatigue and had no time for you. Do not fear, my lovely, the day is young and you can be assured your time will come."

The very thought of this man putting his hands on her made Kathryn want to gag. She would kill herself before she would suffer the abuse this animal had subjected Karen to. A combination of hatred and disgust sent courage to her voice as she met his stare with a glare of her own, and said, "Well, General, since you and your men have finished, the least you can do is help them recover from the wondrous experience, as you call it. Have them taken to a room where they can bathe and provide them with clothing so they might feel like human beings again."

"You have fire in your eyes; I like that in a woman. It signifies that the same such fire burns within your delightful body. I am a lover of fire, my dear, you may be assured of that," laughed Ling. "However, since what you ask is such a small thing, I shall see to it that your request is granted. You may express your gratitude for my kindness when I visit your room later today. I warn you. If you do not please me, you shall endure the same fate as your friend."

Kathryn forced a smile on her lips as she permitted her soft brown eyes to take on a look of false desire, and she replied in a sexy tone, "You will not be disappointed, General, I promise."

The promise in the woman's eyes excited Ling. He called to his guards who came quickly into the room. Waving his hands about in the fashion of one accustomed to giving orders, he shouted for them to clear the room of the drunken officers lying naked among the women. Rooms and baths were to be made ready for the women. The guards saluted and went about their unwanted tasks as Ling turned to Kathryn, bowed, and left the room.

"Kathryn, what are you doing?" whispered Karen, her eyes now staring up at her friend.

"I'm not sure, myself, Karen. But I had to do something. At least you and the others will have a little time to recover form your ordeal. It was all I could think to do."

"He will come for you, Kathryn. You know he will."

"Yes, I know he will, Karen; but I will deal with that when it happens. Right now, I only want to get you and the others upstairs and away from these soldiers before the ordeal begins again. Judging from the looks of some of these guards, that wouldn't take very long. Can you stand up?" she asked.

"I think so. My legs are so sore, and my—my stomach—down there; it hurts so bad, Kathryn."

"I know; come on, it will feel better once we get you in a hot tub," said Kathryn as she helped Karen to her feet and slowly walked her, one step at a time, up the stairs to the very room in which she herself had awakened to find she was in a far different world than the one she had first imagined.

B.J., San, and Lassiter, along with six members of the recon patrol, circled around to the rear of the fortress,

moving quietly though the jungle growth like the tiger
whose home they had invaded. Sergeant Major McKinney,
Crane, and Lieutenant Jacoby with two of San's men and
four Rangers worked their way silently around to the front
of the objective, maintaining a safe distance, and noting the
number of guards and observation positions which guarded
the entrance to Ling's domain. The veteran Rangers immediately realized that gaining entry through the front of the
fortress was going to be difficult.

The problem was that the guards, who rotated at the two
main gates and maintained the outer wall watch towers,
lived in a tented bivouac area located directly in front of the
wall. The jungle growth had been cleared for a distance of
twenty yards all around their tents and the area was clearly
visible to the inner guards who walked the top of the three
story wall. From that height, they had a commanding view
of the jungle and the camp below. Coming out of the jungle
and moving across twenty yards of cleared ground without
being seen or heard was going to be damn near impossible.

B.J. and his group found themselves facing almost the
same problem at the rear of the objective. Not only did they
have a number of soldiers living in makeshift huts and tents,
but also a large number of women and children. San said
some were families of the warlord soldiers; others were
girlfriends or whores from the local villages who lived and
worked at the fortress. There were no major gates at the rear
wall; the only entrance was a single heavy teakwood door at
the east end corner. It was flanked by two machine gun
towers, thirty to thirty-four feet high, containing no fewer
than two guards per tower and sometimes three. B.J. asked
if there were any entrances at the side walls. San told him
there were none. The bandit had been right about one thing;
this was going to be a hard nut to crack—hard for combat
veterans; even harder for young soldiers who had not yet
experienced the baptism of fire. But these were Rangers,
and this was their kind of mission. It was what they had
trained for a hundred times over, going in silently and
swiftly, then coming out hard and loud, taking down
anything or anybody that got in their way. B.J. was

confident in their ability to function as the well oiled machine he knew them to be. His life, as well as the lives of those around them, would depend on that confidence.

Lieutenant General J. J. Johnson and Major General Sweet made their way out the front doors of the crowded airport. Marshall Parsons was waiting for them when they came out; he waved. Opening the tailgate of the Ford Bronco he had borrowed from Colonel Chakkri's headquarters, he took the bags the men were carrying, tossed them into the back, and said, "Good to see you again, Jonathan, only wish it was under better circumstances."

"Me, too, Marsh. General Sweet, this is Marshall Parsons, Chief of Mission and an old friend from my early days of embassy service. Marsh, this is General Raymond Sweet, my deputy."

"My pleasure, sir. We had better get going, John, I have a chopper waiting to fly us up to the border outpost. Figured you would want to get up there right away," said Parsons as he adjusted his glasses and slid in behind the wheel. He started the Bronco and headed out into the congested Thailand traffic.

"I take it you have booked adequate rooms for us at the hotel, Mr. Parsons," said Sweet. Johnson glanced over at his deputy. It seemed a strange question, given the urgency of their situation.

"Of course, General, we are on our way to Colonel Chakkri's headquarters; the chopper is waiting for us there. His staff will see to it that your bags are delivered to your rooms."

Sweet frowned, then looked across at Johnson, "General Johnson, I would prefer to go to the hotel. I'm afraid I have developed a terrible stomach problem during the flight over. I don't think I can last through a helicopter ride; you understand, sir. I only need a few hours to lie down and rest, but don't worry; once I feel better, I'll arrange my own transportation to the border site."

Now it was Johnson's turn to frown, only he couldn't show it. They had only been in Thailand less than thirty minutes and Sweet was already up to something. Johnson didn't know what, but he was sure it wasn't anything that would benefit SOCOM or help the mission. He didn't really want the man at the site, anyway. Perhaps he was really feeling bad; it didn't matter. Johnson did not have the time or the desire to baby-sit another general.

"Marsh, would you mind dropping General Sweet at the hotel?"

"No problem, Jonathan, it's on the way out."

Parsons hurriedly tossed Sweet's bags to the doorman at the hotel and told the man he hoped he would be feeling better soon. He leaped back into the Bronco and took off with Johnson riding in the front seat.

Sweet checked in at the desk and rode up in the elevator with the bellhop carrying his bags. Once in the room, the man placed Sweet's bags on the bed, walked across the room, opened the drapes, and smoothed out a wrinkle that had formed on the bedspread. Sweet watched as the man performed these rituals in order to receive a respectable tip form the guest. For his plan to work, he would need a contact. This was Sweet's first trip to Thailand; he had no idea where to begin. All travelers knew that bellhops and desk clerks knew where to find anything and everything that a guest might require. For a fee, they would even make the arrangements; that seemed simple enough.

The young man finished pressing out the wrinkle, turned with his hand extended, and smiled at Sweet.

"Uh—tell me, boy, would you happen to know where I might be able to acquire something for this pain I'm having in my stomach? It's really quite painful and I know I won't be able to sleep with it like this."

"We have a drugstore in the hotel, sir. If you like I shall—"

"Uh—no, that wasn't what I had in mind. Those chew-able tablets and other junk they sell really don't stop the pain. I had something more—let's say—stronger in mind. Something that might stop the pain and take my mind off any problems I might have, if you know what I mean."

The Thai boy's eyebrow raised an inch or so as he looked again at the general's stars attached to the uniform he had just placed on the bed with the bags. "You say you would like something stronger that makes you feel good, sir; is that right? How good?"

Sweet smiled. "Real good," he said.

"Drug dealing in Thailand is very serious offense, sir. It would require very much money to make the risk worth the reward."

"How much?" asked Sweet.

"Cocaine or heroin?" asked the boy.

"Both."

"One bag apiece, five hundred dollars."

Sweet was taken back by the price but quickly decided it would be money well spent to get even with B.J. Mattson and Jake Mortimer.

"Deal! When can I get it?"

"One hour. You meet me in alley behind the hotel; I have it for you. Now, money, please," said the boy, his hand once again extended.

Sweet pulled five one hundred dollar bills from his wallet and laid them in the boy's hand. The boy counted them, nodded his approval, then left. Removing the small travel alarm clock from his suitcase, Sweet set it for forty-five minutes and stretched out on the bed to get some rest. His thoughts flashed on what he would do his first week as the new Commander of SOCOM, once General Johnson was relieved of his command because he could not control the drug problem among his own officers.

CHAPTER 11

By the time the recon team had returned to the crash site, an increase in the number of personnel was apparent. It continued to grow as more and more small groups of San's army continued to arrive. Jake and Captain Ross, with the aid of two bandit officers who remained behind, kept a running total of the increasing numbers and placed the new arrivals in security positions along the ever expanding perimeter around the downed aircraft. San and B.J. had agreed that it was only a matter of time before the Burmese Government would send ground troops into the area. Helicopters and search planes were already crisscrossing the countryside in an attempt to locate the crash—a job that had been made even more difficult by an outstanding joint effort of camouflaging by the Rangers and the bandits before the recon force had departed. The last thing B.J. needed now was a running gun battle with government troops which could be backed up by a highly proficient Air Force armed with mini-guns, twenty millimeter canons, bombs, rockets, and napalm. He and the Rangers of B Company were in the country illegally; they held no more status now than did General San and his bandits.

The air seemed charged with electricity as intense feelings of anticipation of a coming assault spread throughout the gathering army. B.J. signaled for Captain Ross and

Lieutenant Jacoby to join Jake and him at the side of the aircraft.

"Captain Ross, Jake and I have discussed the upcoming operation. We both agree that because you two gentlemen are the leaders of B Company, and these are your Rangers, men you have commanded, trained with every day, and know better than anyone else possibly could, that you should be the ones to plan and execute this operation," said B.J.

The two Rangers glanced at one another, finding it difficult to hide their feelings of appreciation at B.J.'s suggestion.

"But sir, didn't Colonel Decker say that General Johnson wanted you and Commander Mortimer to be in charge of this deal?" asked Lieutenant Jacoby.

"Lieutenant, Jake and I were sent to Thailand by the Special Operations Command to evaluate the proficiency and effectiveness of B Company, 2nd Battalion of the 75th Rangers. That is exactly what we intend to do; the only difference will be in the grading system. There won't be any red pencils or evaluation books on this exercise; those that fail this exam will fail permanently. Gentlemen, this is your command and those are your people. Jake and I will be available for any assistance you may need in the planning and will perform whatever duties you may select for us in the actual battle plan. This is a Ranger operation, Captain Ross. Take charge."

Ross and Jacoby were smiling ear to ear as both men saluted. Ross replied, "Yes, sir! Airborne!"

B.J. returned the salute and watched the two men as they went about gathering their squad leaders, platoon sergeants, and San and his officers for a strategy meeting. "I'd feel a lot better if we had more combat vets with these guys," said Jake.

"Hell, Jake, where do you think we get combat vets from, anyway? There are only two kinds of Rangers that are going to come out of this thing. Those that survive will be called combat vets; those that don't will be called casualties of war. It's always been that way; I guess it always will."

Lassiter came across the clearing carrying the radio and extended the handset to B.J. He said, "It's General Johnson; he wants to talk to you."

Mattson took the radio and knelt down. "Little Beaver, this is Red Rider One, over."

"Red Rider One, this is Little Beaver Leader. Do you have a positive fix on those members of the tribe that have departed for the happy hunting ground, over?"

"Affirmative. We will send that information by way of the sky god at the end of this transmission, over."

The radio man began setting up the satellite dish and readying the DMDG code burst device and the coded tape for transmission. The tape contained the names of those bodies that had been positively identified.

"Rider one, are the rest of the tribe doing well? Over."

"Negative, negative, we have fourteen that have wandered from the reservation and are presently in bad company. Corrective action is being taken at this time to recover them, over."

"Roger. Understand. Be aware that the big chief and his council are powwowing with the other tribe but have not yet reached an agreement. They are still considered hostile, say again, hostile toward our tribe. Our chief and the full council agree that any and all actions you may have to take to recover our property is totally acceptable to them, over."

B.J. smiled up at Jake, "Sure makes a difference when it's the congressional boys in trouble, don't it, Jake?" Jake grinned and nodded in agreement.

"Roger, Little Beaver. Understand. I have additional information to smoke signal for the sky god. Have included information that we believe needs immediate attention. I have negative further at this time, will keep you informed as to the results of recovery. Do you have anything further for me, over?"

"Negative, Red Rider One. Happy trails, amigo. Little Beaver, out."

B.J. passed the radio to the communications specialist who quickly attached the necessary cables to the radio, keyed in the DMDG code device, and sent the tape. The entire transmission of the three hundred letter group had taken less than five seconds. The information B.J. had referred to was a brief outline of Nickleson's story, a list of the numbers on the card Kendell had given Nickleson when he arrived in Washington, and the full names of the two bodyguards and their social security numbers. One of the numbers Lassiter had found in Rivera's personal effects had matched one of the numbers on the card Nickleson had been given by Kendell. B.J. didn't know if it meant anything; but if he had to risk his ass in Burma, the least the FBI could do was check out those numbers.

General San came up to B.J. "I have two hundred and thirty of my army present, Major B.J. Your Captain Ross say we have big briefing in one hour, if that okey dokey with you."

B.J. laughed and put his hand on San's shoulder as he said, "It be okey dokey with me, General."

Karen Newell was sleeping soundly now; so were the other women Ling had ordered brought to his own room. It was the largest room in the fortress, and this way he could keep them all in one place. They would be easier to guard and he wouldn't have to worry about his officers attempting a repeat performance of the night before. Even his officers were not fool enough to go by themselves among a group of women with a hard-on.

Kathryn stepped quietly to the door and attempted to turn the handle. It was locked. Just as she was about to walk away, she heard Ling's voice as he came down the hall; he was talking with someone. Kathryn placed her ear against the door. She recognized the voice of the man who now spoke to Ling; it was Charles Kendell's voice.

"I swear on my word as a U.S. senator, General Ling; the money is there. All I want in return is to be set free, unharmed. Is that such a hard request to grant me in exchange for two million dollars in cash?"

Ling had thoughtlessly stopped in the hallway directly in front of the room in which the women were sleeping.

Kathryn could hear every word that passed between the two men clearly.

"Ha! Your word as an American politician! You must be mad. I would just as soon take the word of that renegade bandit, San, as yours; at least he is a thief with honor. You Kendell, have no honor at all. You would have me believe that you carry about two million dollars in American money as if it were nothing. You must take me for a fool, Kendell. You tell me this wild tale in the hope that I will take you outside the walls of the fortress so that you may attempt escape."

There were signs of panic in Kendell's voice as he pleaded with the man to believe him.

"No, no, General Ling, I swear to God the money is there. I buried it myself after the crash. My man Alfonso, the man you shot, stood guard while I buried it; you have to believe me."

"Why would anyone, even a senator, find it necessary to have such a large amount of money with him when he travels? Present me with a logical reply if you can; then maybe I will consider your ridiculous story."

Kendell stood quietly staring into the man's coal black eyes. He had not planned on having to go this far, believing that only the mention of money would be enough; but Ling wasn't buying it. Sweat formed on Kendell's face, sending small stinging sensations along the lines of open cuts around his eye and lips. "Come, Kendell, convince me that there is all this money lying in a hole out there in the jungle."

"Do you know of a man called Yang Hwe Khan?" asked Kendell.

Kendell could tell by the change in expression that suddenly came over Ling; the man did know the name. The sarcastic, flippant remarks were gone now. Ling stepped closer; seriousness gripped his face.

"What do you know of Yang Khan? If you lie to me, I shall castrate you right here in this hallway."

"Khan is the drug lord of the eastern edge of the golden triangle located in Laos. The money was from an American drug dealer in Washington who I have been working with for the last three years. The money was to have been delivered to Khan's agents in Bangkok. It was to be the down payment on a shipload of heroin to be smuggled into the United States aboard a freighter. As a member of the drug enforcement committee, I was to establish my own special task force of agents who would actually be men working for the Washington drug dealer. They would stage a raid on the ship, find enough heroin to satisfy the press and anyone else that the raid was successful, then, in the middle of the night, remove the real shipment and transport it into the city. It was quite a plan, actually. It would have worked, too, if only that damn plane hadn't crashed.

"So you see, General Ling, I am not lying to you. There is two million dollars in American money out there; and if we have a deal, I will take you right to it; you can have it all. I only want out of this mess."

Ling had watched the man's eyes as he told his story. It was true that Khan was the powerful warlord to the east. It was also true that he was known to ship large quantities of heroin to the United States. Kendell's story could be true. Only one thing puzzled Ling.

"Tell me, Kendell. After the incident of last night, why would you want to give money to a man who had ordered the sexual assault of your wife? Even now, you talk of only setting yourself free, nothing of your woman. Why is that?"

Kendell could tell that the situation was improving. He attempted a smile as he replied, "I, like you, General Ling, have a large appetite for women. Wanda and I have nothing in common but the title of husband and wife. She had more sex last night than she has had from me in over ten years. Do with her what you will. There are plenty of young women in Washington, General. I will not be alone for long; I can assure you of that."

Ling laughed, showing bright white teeth. "So, I see. Perhaps you and I are not such different men after all, Kendell. We both seek the same things: power, money, and women. To have all three is to have true happiness. Come, we will go find this money. Then possibly we can arrange

for your man in Washington to purchase his heroin from me
next time."

"I didn't know you ran poppy farms in your province,
General."

"I don't, Mr. Kendell; I steal it from those who do."

Both men were laughing at the remark as they moved
down the hall. Kathryn could not believe what she had just
heard. Turning quietly from the door, Kathryn saw Wanda
Kendell standing only a few feet away. Tears were stream-
ing down her face. She, too, had heard the conversation.

The alleyway smelled of dead fish and rotting food.
Sweet pulled a handkerchief from his pocket and placed it to
his nose in a vain attempt to ward off the terrible smell. He
had been waiting in this stink hole for nearly a half hour and
was beginning to believe he had been ripped off. If he had
been, what could he do? He couldn't go to the police and
say, "Excuse me, but I gave a kid five hundred dollars for
some cocaine and heroin, and he didn't come back." Yeah,
that would work. Shit! He had about given up when the
back door swung open and the boy peered out. Seeing
Sweet, he looked up and down both ends of the alleyway;
then came outside.

"About damn time." growled Sweet.

"So sorry, sir. Had very hard time finding dealer," said
the boy as he pulled the two small envelopes from his shirt
pocket, opened them, and held them out to Sweet who had
no idea what the boy was doing. "You try, make sure it
number one stuff."

"Oh—uh—yes, of course." Sweet didn't know a thing
about drugs, but he had watched a lot of *Miami Vice* with
Crockett and Tubbs. Taking one of the small packets in his
hand, he wet a finger and dipped it into the white powder.
Seeing the boy's look of approval, he licked the powder
from his fingertip. It left a bitter taste in his mouth as he
said, "Oh, yes, this will be fine." He quickly closed both
envelopes, foregoing a taste of the second one. "Now, my
little friend, I need one more favor."

"I do not do favors, sir," replied the boy slyly, indicating that everything cost money.

"How much for you to get me the key to a certain room here at the hotel?"

"Which room?"

"I'm not sure. If I give you the names, you can find out and get me those keys. Okay?"

"One hundred dollars, American," said the boy.

"That's damn highway robbery," exploded Sweet.

The boy shrugged his shoulders and smiled as he said, "Hey, it's no sweat off my balls; you're the one who wants the keys."

The little bastard had him and he knew it, thought Sweet. "Okay," he said as he pulled a hundred dollars from his wallet. "Bring them to my room when you get them." He hurriedly scribbled the names on a piece of paper and gave them to the boy along with the money. "Try and hurry this time, will you?"

The boy shoved the money into his pocket and went back inside. Sweet followed him a few minutes later and went to his room to wait. Now all he had to do was plant the drugs, then get a ride to the outpost. Everything would be in place when they returned.

Captain Ross seemed worried as he prepared to give the briefing for the operation. B.J. had only made one suggestion during the initial planning. That had involved the use of the Steyr sniper rifles with the silencers to take down the guards on the wall, should they detect the teams moving toward the gates. What was bothering Ross now was the total number of enemy they could expect to encounter once inside the fortress. The only numbers he had right now were for those outside the walls. San had noted the problem and had reassured Ross that he would have the numbers by the time the briefing started. It was time, and still nothing. San told him to go ahead and start. By the time he reached that part of the briefing, he would have his count.

The Rangers and San's officers gathered near the plane as Ross stepped forward and pulled a blanket from the bare metal on the side of the plane. A diagram of the fortress had been drawn on the metal with a heavy black dye that Ross had made from the juice of the Indian almond and charcoal. Ross had just begun to give the operations order when he suddenly paused and stared at the back of the crowd. B.J. and Jake turned to see what had caused the halt in the briefing. "Well, I'll be damned," whispered B.J. as he made his way through the troops and toward the two bandits who were leading an old man and his burro into the clearing. San rushed forward and waved for the guard to return to their positions as he stepped forward and embraced the old man. Lassiter stood next to B.J. "That old guy look familiar?" he asked.

"Yeah, same man, same burro," he answered as San led the old man up to B.J.

"Major, I am honored to have you meet my grandfather," smiled San.

The old man placed his hands together and bowed as he spoke in flawless English, "It is my pleasure, Major. You and your men scared the hell out of me on that trail last night; and your young friend here could use more practice on his Burmese."

Lassiter nearly blushed, as a stunned B.J. said, "I'm—I mean, we're sorry about that, sir."

"Apology accepted, Major. Now, let us get down to business. I have just come from the fortress. You are more fortunate than you know. There are fewer than three hundred of Ling's entire army at that evil place. Most are scattered throughout the province collecting taxes for the bastard. They will not return for at least two days. If you plan to strike at the snake, now is the time."

"Did you have a chance to see any of the Americans, sir?" asked B.J.

"My name is, Than, Major; no need to know the rest, it is too long and you would forget it anyway. Yes, I saw two; both were men. One they brought from the fortress; he was dead. The soldiers tossed his body over the small cliff to the west of the fortress. The other was an older man. He appeared to have been beaten about the face, but yet he was speaking with Ling as if they were old friends. I found that strange, but then I am old and many things seem strange to me now."

"What about the women?" asked Lassiter.

For the first time, B.J. saw the old man's eyes change. It was a sad look. "I did not see them, but heard talk among the soldiers and the women outside the wall. They heard screaming that seemed to last the entire night. Some spoke of a wild orgy involving Ling and his officers. I do not know if these things are true; but as my grandson will tell you, Ling is a cruel and sadistic man. I would not put such things beyond his madness."

Slow whispers made their way through the ranks of the young Rangers as the word of the possible rape was passed from man to man. B.J. thought of Nickleson and his young wife. He saw no need to mention the possibility that what Than said was true.

"Major, if I may ask, how do you plan to get past the women and children and into the fortress without someone shouting out a warning?" asked Than.

"It's not going to be easy, Than. There are a lot of people in those camps."

"I know, Major. Many are only simple people that have nowhere else to go. I fear that they shall be caught in the crossfire should you be discovered. Many will surely die, especially the small children."

"I'm afraid you're right, Than, but we have to get our people out of there. You yourself heard what they are doing to them. I don't see any other way," said B.J. with marked sadness. "If we try to sneak in and move them out before the shooting starts, someone is bound to warn the soldiers."

Than cast his eyes to the ground. He knew B.J. was right.

"Major, what if they were all asleep? You know, how you say, knocked up?" asked San.

"You mean knocked out."

"Yes." San turned to his grandfather. "The sleeping juice from the river vine, grandfather. The people at the fortress draw their water from the well at the front gates. If we place the liquid into the well, we could wait until nighttime for it to put them to sleep. Then should we have to fire our weapons, at least they would not be running wildly among the bullets."

Than's face lit up with new hope as he asked, "Could we do such a thing, Major? Would you be willing to wait a few more hours to start your attack?"

B.J. looked around at the faces of the Rangers who would have to fight this battle. Their faces showed the answer. Ross and Jacoby nodded their approval. "Yes, Than, we will wait if it means saving innocent lives. There will be enough dying tonight."

Than told his grandson to give him twenty men to help pick the vines. Five were to leave their weapons there; they would be going into the camp with him to help put the sleeping liquid into the well. San shouted orders and Than bowed once more to the Americans before turning to his burro and heading for the river.

B.J. walked over to Ross. "Sorry about the change in plans, Captain; but if it's any comfort to you, I give you a hundred out of a possible hundred for mission prep."

"Thanks, Major. Guess this is what they mean when they put those words, 'Officer is highly flexible,' in an efficiency report."

It was 1600 hours when one of the men who had left with Than returned with news that all had gone as planned at the well. However, there had been some activity going on inside the fortress. They had overheard one of the soldiers cursing because he was going to have to go with his company on another trek into the jungle. From the way he had talked, Ling himself might be going out with them; the man wasn't sure. B.J. and the others welcomed the news; it meant there would be even fewer soldiers inside the fortress. San suggested that he send two of his men to count the number of soldiers leaving as they came out the gates. It was a good idea. The men were sent on their way with instructions to report back to San, who would already be in position near the west cliffs with a force of seventy-five men, Lassiter included.

Jake, Lieutenant Jacoby, and Sergeant Major McKinney would be positioned to the east, with a force of twenty Rangers and fifty bandits, while B.J., Ross, and Crane would move to the front to take the fortress head-on with eighty Rangers and bandits. The MX 3000 team radios had been checked and call signs designated for each element of the attack force. General San was Gray Fox Three; Jake, Gray Fox Two; and B.J., Gray Fox One. Each element was carrying one of the sniper rifles. Ross, B.J., and Crane were carrying the silencers for the 9mm pistols. They would be the element that would be conducting the up-close and personal work. Once the mission began, there could be no turning back; the prisoners were the primary concern. No matter what else was happening in another part of the fortress, the prisoners came foremost. Once they had been located and freed, the securing element would take them straight out of the fortress and head directly for the Salween River. They would follow it south for one hour. They were not to stop for any reason. Congressman Nickleson was being carried on a litter. Ten bandits as security had already been sent to the river. They would link up with the other prisoners and the securing element for the move south. The remaining elements, upon receiving confirmation that all prisoners were accounted for, would then withdraw and fight a rear guard action to forestall any pursuit. They were as ready as they were going to be as Captain Ross checked his watch, looked out over the men who had been entrusted to his care, and said, "Okay, Rangers! Let's get it done."

There were no cheers this time. Cheering was for football games and remembering your first piece of ass. Now, there were only the serious, camouflaged faces of a group of determined men who had a purpose as they silently answered Ross's challenge. One by one they broke off into their groups and faded into a jungle that was slowly being covered by the black veil of night. For some, it would be the veil of death.

Charles Kendell watched with idle curiosity as the women of the tent city at the front of the fortress tossed their wooden buckets into the gaping hole of the well. They retrieved their buckets with a grace that highlighted their firm breasts which strained against the colorful material of their thin blouses. General Ling, dressed smartly in a freshly pressed set of camouflaged jungle fatigues, came out of the gates. He was followed by four of his officers and a contingent of fifty men, all heavily armed.

Stepping in front of Kendell, Ling noticed the lustful look in the man's eyes as he watched the women at the well. Smiling briskly, he said, "Once we have recovered the money, perhaps you would like to join me with a few of those ladies, Kendell."

"I just might take you up on that, General Ling. It has been a while since I've had the old pipes blown out," laughed Kendell, the pain in his face forgotten.

"Even better, if you like, I shall let you have the woman they call Nickleson, after I have finished with her, of course. I had planned to educate the young woman in the ways of the world this afternoon, but there is no hurry. There will be time when we return. Come, let us go."

Now, there was an idea, thought Kendell as he followed Ling. A romp in the hay with Edward Nickleson's lovely new bride of only one month. She did have a nice body. Why not? Hell, she might even like it. The thought of her naked before him stirred a reaction. He suddenly felt himself getting an erection. He was right; it had been too long. Kendell smiled at the old man with the burro as they rounded the corner of the stone wall and headed into the jungle.

CHAPTER 12

Lassiter placed the headset with the whisper mike over his ears. Switching the hand-held radio to the voice-activated position, he began his call; "Gray Fox One, this is Gray Fox Three."

B.J.'s voice came through the small earpiece crystal clear, "Gray Fox Three, this is Gray Fox One. Go."

"Gray One, Gray Two, we have a report of fifty; I say again, fifty personnel have departed objective. General Ling and one American. It appears to be the same one Than told us about. How copy?"

"Roger, good, copy. Fox Three, have you sighted in on your targets yet?"

"Negative; will do that now; Fox Three, out."

Lassiter motioned for San to pass him the sniper rifle with the scope. Placing the butt of the .308 caliber weapon firmly in the crook of his shoulder, Lassiter reached forward and activated the infrared system. Squinting his eye, he placed it against the soft rubber piece that sat at the end of the scope and aligned the cross hairs on the chest of one of the soldiers standing on top of the wall. Satisfied that he had his spot, he then activated the computerized distance scanner and watched as a series of digital numbers changed rapidly at the upper left-hand corner of the scope. Gradually the numbers began to slow and finally lock on to one number. The target was exactly 216 yards from his position.

Allowing for dip and minimal loss of muzzle velocity caused by the weight of the silencer, he readjusted the sight once more; then he laid the rifle aside. He was ready.

B.J. lowered the PVS night vision glasses and nodded to Ross. The water had done its job. Even the three scraggly dogs that they had spotted earlier were out. "Fox Two, Fox Three, this is Fox One," whispered Ross into the small, highly sensitive mike.

"Fox Two, go."

"Fox Three, go."

"Fox Two and Three, this is One; we're going in, Fox One, out."

Captain Ross motioned for Sergeant Crane to begin moving for the tents. Crane, clutching the silenced Beretta in his hand, and hugging the ground, slowly pushed off with his right foot and began to snake his way toward the first tent. Three Rangers followed in like fashion. At the same moment, B.J. began inching his way forward on the left. Ross took the middle. The movement was painstakingly slow but necessarily so, one mistake and all hell could break loose. Sweat flowed freely from the faces of the men who now closed in on the first row of tents. Lifting the flap only inches from the ground, B.J. stared inside. An old man, three women, and four children were sound asleep. Lowering the flap, he signaled that his objective was clear, and he swung out around the canvas. Still moving on his belly like a snake, he headed for the next row. One by one each tent was checked until the three men in the lead were now on line beyond the camp. Across the open ground, twenty yards in front of them were the huge teakwood gates. Three soldiers sat on the ground, their backs against the wall. They were asleep. Directly in front of the gate another four men were smoking and talking in whispers. Ross signaled that he would take the two men in the middle; B.J. and Crane would take down the two on the outside. Raising his Beretta and steadying it in both hands, Ross slowly took up the slack on the hair trigger. He pulled off four rapid shots and the two men in the middle suddenly slumped backward and fell to the ground. Ross heard the phwffff, phwffff of the silencers as he watched the two outside men jerk and grab their chests as they fell quietly to the ground.

B.J. looked to the top of the wall. The guards never broke stride; they had not heard a thing. Ross motioned again and the line of men began crawling toward the gates. This was the place that B.J. had feared would be a problem. They had to cover twenty yards of open ground without being seen by the men on the wall; they hoped that no one came out the gates unexpectedly. One shot and they would be ducks in the water for the men three stories above them.

As if by ordained premonition, B.J. froze. Three soldiers had just come around the east corner of the wall, while another two suddenly appeared at the corner of the west wall. Half of the Rangers were strung out in the open while the others were still at the edge of the camp. Crane shifted his Beretta in the direction of the three to the east; it was no good; the distance was too great for any kind of accurate kill shot. A wounded man could still fire a warning shot. Any second now one group or the other was going to see the bodies piled in front of the gate. The three coming from the east were the first to see something was wrong. Luckily, they didn't start yelling; however, they broke in a dead run for the gates. B.J. tensed, expecting a scream or a rifle shot to bring a hail of bullets down from the wall. Instead, he saw the third man, the second, and finally the first turn and slam into the wall.

The two on the west end stood like stone statues, confused by what they had just seen. It was long enough for Lassiter to take his shots. The first blew out the side of one man's head. His friend had opened his mouth to scream but nothing but blood came out as the kid's second shot struck the man at the base of the skull; the .308 round nearly took the man's head off at the shoulders. "You owe me one, sucker," came the whispered voice of Jake Mortimer who had snapped off the three shots that had taken out the men to the east.

Ross breathed a sigh of relief and began the crawl once again. Finally, they were out of sight of the guards on top and among the still warm bodies at the gate. Pulling a shirt and hat from one of the dead men, B.J. passed it to the bandit who had been with Crane. The man quickly slipped into the half uniform and positioned the hat. He removed a bottle of wine from the bag he had been carrying. Standing in front of the gate, he reached up and knocked on the security hatch located in the very center of one of the double doors. The guard inside opened the hatch and asked what he wanted. Holding the bottle so it could be seen, the bandit said they had already drunk too much, and they wanted him to have the extra bottle. The man inside hesitated only for a moment. B.J. and the others heard a heavy metal bolt being pulled aside. They got to their feet, Ross and B.J. behind the bandit, Crane in the shadow of the other. As the door opened and the man stepped out to take the bottle, Crane extended his arm, and with the barrel of the pistol only inches from the man's head, squeezed off one round. The guard tossed forward into the bandit's arms and slipped to the ground.

Crane quickly stepped through the gates, followed by B.J. and Ross. They caught four of the guards sitting at a small table to the left; the Berettas bucked and the four pitched backward off their chairs. The bandit at the gate now swung the teakwood doors open wide. This was the signal for Lassiter, Jake, and one of the Rangers at the front to start knocking the guards who were walking the top wall off their perches. They were right on time. The bodies began to fall with a heavy sound as they made the long fall from the three story height and impacted with the hard dirt of the courtyard.

Everything seemed to happen at once now. Ross's element, which had been waiting in the camp, leaped to their feet and made the dash across the open ground, through the gates, and into the courtyard. To the rear of the fortress, Jake and his men found it surprisingly easy to gain entry. Most of those inside were asleep, thanks to the two buckets of water that were sitting on a table near their sleeping area. They were a full two minutes into the attack before the first ear-shattering sounds of automatic weapons firing echoed through the night air. It was the sound of a Russian AK-47;

it had come from an open-air kitchen that had been built in
the corner of the west wall. Two Rangers and one of San's
men lay dead in the dirt. The burst of automatic weapons
fire caught them flat-footed and in the open.

Three Rangers converged on the small area and laid down
a withering hail of automatic fire. The soldier, in a moment
of panic, tried to change positions. It was a bad decision on
his part. One of the Rangers was carrying a 203 and had just
locked a 40mm grenade in place when the man stood up to
make his move; the Ranger fired; the grenade hit the man
square in the chest and exploded, tearing the soldier in half.

The sounds of automatic weapons fire steadily increased
now, as more and more of the soldiers grabbed their
weapons and ran out into the fight. Grenade explosions
rocked the compound and sent white hot metal and rocks
into the air to mingle with the flying lead. In the center of
the courtyard, Rangers, having no time to reload, were
going hand to hand with the soldiers using knives or just
their bare hands against machetes. Men were screaming and
dying all around the fortress. Ross and B.J. rushed toward
the stairs that led up to the main house. A line of AK rounds
tore up the ground behind them. B.J. fired off four quick
rounds, catching a man at the top of the steps in the chest
and sending him over the railing into the garden below.

Sergeant Major McKinney reached the stairs as Ross was
trying to reload. Seeing a soldier coming from under the
steps with a twelve-gauge riot gun aimed at Ross, he
screamed, "Captain!" as he shoved his commander out of
the way and tried to bring his weapon up in time. It was too
late. The shotgun roared, and McKinney took the full force
of the blast in the gut. The impact propelled him three feet
into the air. He died instantly. Ross screamed with rage as
he threw his empty weapon down and leaped over the
railing and on top of the man with the shotgun, sending
them both crashing to the ground. They struggled for a
moment, then Ross pulled the shotgun from the man's
hands and began smashing the butt of the weapon into the
soldier's face until it was nothing but a bloody hole.
Grabbing the bag of shells from beside the body, he loaded

the shotgun and stepped back out from beneath the stair-well. A Chinese soldier was standing only a few feet from him, his back to Ross; he was raising his rifle to fire when Ross yelled, "Hey!" The startled man turned, and Ross blew the top of his head off.

Jake and Lieutenant Jacoby hit the back stairs at a dead run, firing their MP-5 machine guns every step of the way, taking down four Chinese at the top of the stairs. "Loading," yelled Jake. Jacoby automatically stopped and covered Jake while he slammed another magazine into the well. "Okay! Go!" screamed Jake. Both men dashed along the balcony, taking out two more Chinese as they rounded the corner.

General San and Lassiter moved their group in from the west, splitting their forces. San positioned half of them in front of the fortress to serve as a blocking force, while Lassiter and the others raced around to the rear wall and did the same. The maneuver served a dual purpose. It cut off escape routes for Ling's soldiers that were inside and at the same time, it kept any unexpected guests from getting inside. The wisdom of the tactic was proven only moments later as a Chinese officer rallied forty soldiers at the far end of the courtyard. In a wild, desperate charge for the gate and escape, they ran the gauntlet of withering fire being laid down by the Rangers. Thirteen soldiers and the officer survived the suicidal charge, only to be cut to pieces in a hailstorm of lead as they burst past the gate and straight into the waiting guns of San's blocking force.

Red tracers ricocheted off stone walls and spiraled skyward, making wild, twisting patterns until they disap-peared into the night. Showers of sparks chased the ssssshhh sounds of parachute flares as they climbed into the darkness, popped, and exploded into bright lights that hung aloft by small parachutes that now drifted slowly down; each casting an eerie yellow glow over the killing and mayhem taking place below.

The women in Ling's room were huddled together near the bed. One of their number lay in the center of the floor; a crimson stain spread the width of her chest. She had been standing, looking out the window when the battle started. There had been no shattering of glass, only a low, almost musical plink as the small 5.56 round punched a perfectly round hole through the window pane and struck the young woman in the heart. She was dead before she hit the floor. Ling's men were shouting and running up and down the hallway. Kathryn, Wanda, and Karen held each other's trembling hands. There was panic in their eyes and fear in their hearts. They had no idea what was going on beyond the locked door of the room.

Suddenly the doorknob began to twist back and forth. Someone was trying to get in. There were more frantic twists of the handle as others beat on the heavy door in a futile attempt to find a way past the dead-bolt that held it tightly secured. Someone screamed an order in Chinese and the twisting and pounding stopped.

"Maybe they're gone," said Wanda quietly. "I'll—"

A sudden burst of automatic fire tore through the door, splintering the wood around the lock. Two heavy kicks and the door flew open.

"Oh, my God!" cried Wanda. She recognized the Chinese officer who entered the room. He had been the first to rape her the night before. Two soldiers with long black rifles followed him into the room.

"Come, American bitches! Your soldiers will not fire with you in front of us. Come, I say!"

The hellish sounds of the battle that was raging outside sounded even louder with the door standing open.

"No!" screamed Kathryn. "We're not going out there."

Cursing, the officer singled out one of the soldiers and told him to shoot one of the women—any one—it didn't matter. The soldier raised the barrel of the rifle, and with a morbid grin on his face, aimed the weapon at Wanda Kendell's head.

"No! no! We'll go, we'll go," cried Kathryn.

A deafening shot rang out. Wanda fainted at the sight of the blood that exploded outward from the grinning soldier's chest. The impact sent him off his feet and halfway across the room. The officer, shocked for a moment by the sudden action, turned quickly toward the door. He only had time to hear the pump-slide action of another twelve-gauge slug going into the chamber of the shotgun before it exploded and tore away his right eye and jawbone. The next round ripped off his arm before he went down. Two more rapid pumps brought ear-shattering explosions that sent the last soldier ricocheting off the wall and over the bed into the screaming group of blood-spattered women.

Ross was thumbing more loads into the shotgun. B.J. went spread-eagle on the floor and squeezed off three quick rounds forming a triangle over the right shirt pocket of a soldier running down the hall.

"B.J., they're in here!" yelled Ross, as he took up a position by the door, the shotgun at the ready. Mattson scrambled to his feet, ran into the room, cast a glance at the dead woman on the floor, and went around the bed. There, huddled in the corner, clinging to each other with their heads down, were the six sole surviving women of this nightmare. Lowering his rifle, B.J. stepped forward and knelt near them. His voice was soft as he asked, "Which one of you ladies is Mrs. Nickleson?"

Kathryn slowly raised her head and looked into the sweat streaked camouflaged face of the big American. B.J. recognized the big brown eyes. They were the same eyes that had mesmerized him on the CNN News report. There couldn't be two sets of eyes that beautiful. Reaching out a big hand that was covered with sweat and traces of splattered blood, B.J. said, "Come on, Kathryn, it's time to go back to Iowa."

Kathryn hesitated to touch the hand. She feared that this wasn't really happening and that touching the hand would make this man with the caring voice and soft eyes disappear.

"Let's go, Kathryn. Your husband won't appreciate me keeping you out late on our first date," said B.J. with a heartwarming smile.

Kathryn's eyes lit up. "He's alive? Edward is alive?"

"Yes, he's hurt, but doing fine. I promised him I'd bring

you home, Kathryn. However, the longer we sit here, the harder it gets. Let's go, ladies."

The women were all crying with joy. Wanda reached out her chubby arms and pulled B.J.'s head to her and kissed his cheek, camouflage and all, as she cried, "Oh, God bless you."

"Thank you, Ma'am. I need all the blessing I can get these days. Now, up and at 'em. We're not out of this yet." The sudden explosion of the shotgun as Ross killed a soldier coming out of the room across the hall emphasized B.J.'s statement. Moving the women to the door, he held them back as Ross went out into the hall and cautiously made his way to the end of the corridor. Satisfied that it was clear, he waved to B.J., who led the group into the blood covered hallway and along one wall. The radio hanging from his web gear came to life. "Fox One, Fox Two, over." It was Jake.

"Two, this is One, go."

B.J. could tell by Jake's short breaths as he talked that he had been running. "One—this is—Two. We—found six, say again, six males and have extracted them to—to a position near the gate. Have you located the other half of the package? Over."

"Roger, Fox Two. We are on our way out now. Will meet you at the gate. Fox One, out." B.J. snapped the radio back in place and turned to the women. "Okay, ladies, from here on out it gets fast and furious. I want you to hold onto to each other's hands and stay in single file; don't bunch up. We're going to be running, so try to keep your balance and don't fall. If you do, don't worry; we're not going to leave anybody. Just get up as fast as you can and join hands again. Okay?"

They nodded that they understood. Their eyes still held that frightened look, but there was also a glint of hope in them. "Okay, then, ladies, hold hands." B.J. waited until they had their hands tightly locked together; then reaching down and taking Kathryn's warm hand into his own, he said, "Let's do it." They broke away from the wall and began running for the stairway. Ross was already moving down the steps; the shotgun ready to clear a path through hell itself, if necessary.

Outside, the Rangers had secured the machine gun towers and wrecked havoc on the confused warlord soldiers. Over one hundred bodies littered the steps and courtyard of the fortress. They hadn't wiped out all the soldiers yet. A group of about fifty had locked themselves in a wine cellar at the far end of the compound and were firing a shot every now and then, not hitting anyone. For now, the Rangers were in total control.

B.J., Ross, and the women linked up with Jake at the gate. The rescued hugged and held each other. B.J. turned to Ross and said, "Captain, I request permission to remain with the rear guard element while the rest of you get your lovely asses out of here."

"You got it, Major. Jake, get the survivors moving; my element will take the point. We'll keep the women and the others in the middle and let San bring up the rear. B.J., how long will you have to hold here?"

"I'll give you thirty minutes' lead time. We kicked the shit out of these boys; I don't think they'll be in any hurry to come after us."

"Okay, give me a call when you fall back, and I'll let San know you're coming up behind him. Let's go, Jake."

Mortimer stepped forward and slapped B.J. on the shoulder. "That boy handles this command business pretty well; wouldn't be surprised to see him make general one day."

"You should see how he handles that shotgun. Listen, Jake, watch your ass out there. Remember, Ling's running around somewhere with fifty men, and I'm sure he's heard all the racket and seen the fireworks. He's going to be one very pissed off Chinaman. You might want to remind Ross of that."

"I will." Jake paused. There was true feeling in his voice as he looked at Mattson, "B.J., when this is over, I really hope you and Charlotte can work something out. You're both kind of special people to me."

Mattson smiled. "Better get out of here before somebody signs you up to write a Dear Abby column."

Mortimer gave his partner a squeeze on the shoulder and winked as he turned and walked away. B.J. had made a joke out of it, but Jake had seen the same hope in his partner's eyes.

Ross gathered his well-armed caravan together and made a quick check of the Rangers. Eleven had been killed and thirteen wounded, four seriously. The medics had already put the wounded on makeshift litters and started them on plasma. The bodies of the dead remained where they had fallen. Once normal relations were reestablished with the Burmese government, they would be returned to the United States for burial with military honors.

Lassiter joined B.J. as the column disappeared into the jungle.

"Well, looks like we pulled it off, B.J. Another four or five hours and they'll be safe inside Thailand."

"A lot can happen in four or five hours, Adam; and like they say, "It ain't over till it's over. We still got those guys in the wine cellar?"

"Yeah."

"Take a couple of the boys and all the C-4 plastic explosives you can find. Wire up the door to blow if they try to get out, then hustle back here. I told Ross we'd be pulling out in thirty minutes, and I don't want to be late."

"You got it," said Lassiter as he pointed to two men and left.

Mattson looked at his watch and grinned. Parsons would be proud of him; for once in his life, he was actually concerned about being somewhere on time.

At the first sound of gunfire, General Ling had moved his forces to the side of a hill where he could get a better view of his beloved fortress. The tracers, parachute flares, and explosions told him that his men were under heavy attack by a force far larger than the one he now had. He could not afford to go charging recklessly back to help his belea- guered army. He did not know the enemy's strength nor their disposition around the fortress. He could only wait until daylight and hope that his army could hold off the attackers. Kendell stood silently beside the general. His eyes fixed on the dull yellow lights that swung in the night sky and their slow descent into the jungle beyond. This affair served only to give the senator more confidence that his luck had finally changed. He could have been at the fortress when this attack started rather than safe with Ling and his men.

"Damn Burmese Army," muttered Ling under his breath. "Their generals were paid their money this month. Someone will lose his head over this; that I can promise you." Ling lowered the field glasses in disgust, and with bitterness said, "Come, we can do nothing now; we will go on to the plane and the money."

Following Ling down the side of the hill, Kendell smiled to himself as he thought of the general's remark about payoffs. Whether in Washington or in Burma, it was the same all over, be it warlord or senator, the ascent to power was money.

Johnson was standing at a map board with Colonel Decker and Colonel Chakkri. Chakkri was about to point out the Salweem River when the radio operator sat straight up and uttered, "Oh, shit!" The remark brought perfect silence to the room.

"What is it, Sergeant?" asked Johnson as the group moved across the room and stood near the bank of communications equipment.

The radio operator pulled the headset from his head and turned to Johnson, "I've been picking up a lot of radio traffic from the Burmese, sir. One of their night patrols just reported a major battle in progress near a place called Mong Ton. They say it's lighting up the sky. They're moving that way and want the Air Force to scramble some birds in the air. Sir, if that's our people, they'll get creamed by an air strike."

"Can you raise Red Rider One on that thing?" asked Johnson, the concern clear in his voice.

The sergeant began the call up as Chakkri and Johnson went back to the map. The Thai colonel found the location and nodded his head. "Just as I thought. General Chin Tu Ling has a headquarters not far from the village of Mong Ton; he must have been holding the passengers there. Your Rangers have launched an assault to free them."

The sergeant turned back to General Johnson. "It's no good, sir, they're not answering the call-up. What do you want me to do?"

Johnson hung his head as he softly said, "Pray, Sergeant. That's all we can do."

Lassiter wired the explosives to the door and along the lower part of the outer walls of the wine cellar. He estimated the distance from the handle to the pull release device he had rigged to the main charge. The door opened inward, so he placed the tension on the trigger so that movement of the handle one inch would set off the blast. Those not killed outright would suffer an ear-shattering concussion from the shock that would follow. Outside the wall, B.J. waited for Lassiter. He had insisted that Captain Ross take all of the Rangers with him. He, Lassiter, and thirty bandits would handle the delaying action. For now, Ling's soldiers had had enough of battle. Most, like those in the cellar, had found themselves a place to hide and wait to see what happened next. The few foolish enough to fire an occasional shot quickly found themselves dodging bullets and 40mm grenades.

Lassiter and two bandits broke through the archway of the gates at a dead run. The kid gave B.J. a thumbs-up as he reached the perimeter and knelt beside him. Mattson glanced at his watch; Ross had a forty minute head start. "Round up the rest of the boys and get them moving. I'll keep five with me to cover your withdrawal. We'll give you a five minute lead, and I'll radio Ross that we're pulling out," said B.J. to Lassiter.

Lassiter nodded, then singled out five men to remain with B.J., and retreated with the rest. Mattson placed the thin wired headset and whisper mike over his head and hit the press-to-talk button, "Fox One Alpha, this is Fox One, over."

"Fox One, Fox One Alpha, over." Ross's reply was immediate.

"Alpha, this is One, we are departing the area at this time, over."

"Roger, copy, One. Any problems? Over."

"Negative, we have—" The words had no sooner come from Mattson's lips, than suddenly the jungle behind him erupted into a series of rapid explosions and wild automatic fire. Lassiter was in trouble. Locking the talk button down so that he could have his hands free, B.J. sprang to his feet and raced in the direction of the firefight. Speaking into the mike that hung only one inch from his mouth as he ran, he said, "Correction Alpha One, we have contact. Alpha Three is engaged at this time."

"Do you want our assistance?" asked Ross.

"Negative! Negative! We'll take care of it. You have your mission, One Alpha, and no matter what happens here, you will keep moving. That's an order. You don't stop for anything or anybody. Is that understood?"

"Roger, Fox One. Good luck, B.J., Alpha One, out."

Pulling the headset from his head, B.J. stuffed it into the cargo pocket of his fatigues as he placed the selector switch on his MP-5 to full automatic. The bandits were directly behind and keeping pace with him. B.J.'s first thought was of Ling and the men who had left the fortress earlier in the afternoon. Lassiter must have stumbled into them and a firefight had started. That theory vanished as his boot caught something in the trail and he fell. The bandits immediately stopped, went down on one knee, and formed a circle around the fallen American. B.J. raised himself up onto his elbows and found himself staring into the face of a dead Burmese government soldier. "Shit," he muttered, "Just what we needed, somebody else to shoot at our ass."

The battle had stopped, and the jungle had reverted to it's eerie silence. One of the bandits, a kid named Hung who spoke broken English, tapped Mattson on the arm and pointed to their right. The unmistakable sound of cloth against jungle brush signaled that someone was coming. All guns swung in the direction of the sound, and they waited.

Two of the men who had been with Lassiter pushed their way into the open. They were both covered with blood and were dragging Adam Lassiter by his arms between them. B.J. and the others rushed to help them. Lassiter fell into Mattson's arms. He laid the boy down gently on the damp jungle floor. Blood covered the left side of the kid's head and neck. There were three blood soaked spots spread across his chest. B.J. began undoing the buttons on Lassiter's shirt, silently cursing himself for not having been with the boy when this had happened. Hung knelt down next to him, "One man die; other not live long. He say Burmese army patrol, maybe twenty, thirty men. They no see Army men; Army men no see them; they turn on trail; all see everybody; same time—everybody shoot. Most all, both sides die; Army men run away. He say, one Burmese talky, talky on radio before he die." Hung paused and stared down at Lassiter, "Is too bad; he good man. I sorry, Major."

Hung left B.J. with his friend and motioned for the others to form a security circle around the Americans. B.J. was undoing the last button on the shirt when he felt Lassiter's hand touch his wrist.

"Don't waste—your time, B.J.," Lassiter's voice was weak and racked with pain. Mattson pulled a morphine vial from his pocket, broke the seal on the small 5cc tube, and pushed the needle of the painkiller into the boy's arm. He knew you weren't supposed to give morphine to a man with a head injury. Hell, he was a medic; he knew that; but being a medic, he knew that in this case it didn't really matter. Adam Lassiter was dying and this only made it less painful.

"Thanks, B.J. I thought I could hang—without that— but, God, it hurts—"

Tears were welling up in Mattson's eyes. His voice cracked slightly as he squeezed the boy's hand and replied, "Sure ain't like stubbing a toe, is it, kid?"

Lassiter managed a weak smile, "You're just—like my old man, B.J.; he'd always try to say—something funny when I'd get—hurt. You and—he—would get along—great if—" The boy's face tightened as he coughed. Blood dribbled from the corner of his mouth and down his chin. He gripped B.J.'s hand tightly as he whispered, "B.J., you—go see him—tell him—No telegrams; he deserves— better than—that; you tell him how I—died. Promise me, B.J.—please."

A tear moved slowly down Mattson's cheek, "I promise, kid."

Lassiter's body tensed, the eyes began to roll back as the body drew one last breath. Young Adam Lassiter uttered one last word: "Dad."

Ling's face was livid with rage. The pulsing veins in his neck were clearly visible as he screamed at Kendell, "You bastard of a Yankee dog. I shall skin you alive myself when we return."

The senator lay huddled on the ground; his arm poised to block any further blows from Ling's boots, as he cried, "But it was here. I swear to God, it was right here. I buried it myself. They must have found it. They've taken it with them. You have to believe me, please, General."

"They!" screamed Ling, "Who in hell are they?"

"I don't know," whimpered Kendell.

Ling's boot lashed out, striking Kendell in the shoulder, sending a paralyzing pain shooting down the length of his arm. "You lie, Kendell. Why would anyone who had uncovered two million dollars waste the time to refill a worthless hole in the middle of a jungle? I tell you why. Because there never was any money! I know not what plan you had to bring me out here, but rest assured; you will beg to die a hundred times before the end comes." Ling turned to two of his soldiers. "Get the fool on his feet and tie him. We have wasted enough time on this matter. We return to headquarters. I must see what damage has been done. Then I will deal with this bastard."

Kendell was pulled to his feet as the general stomped off with his army following close behind him. The two soldiers who had the task of caring for the senator cursed him as they cut a vine and began wrapping his hands tightly, watching the last man in the column disappear into the jungle. One soldier slapped Kendell; because of him, they would now have to bring up the rear of the column.

B.J. pressed himself closer to the ground as Ling and his army passed. If it had not been for the ranting and raving of the general, B.J. and his men would have walked straight into the group around the plane. Hung touched B.J.'s arm and nodded back up the small trail made by Ling's army. His eyes widened as he saw the American being pushed and shoved ahead of the two soldiers.

The knife was in his hand before he knew it. Hung now had his knife, too. He smiled as he pointed to the first soldier, then to himself. There was no time to reply. Springing up like a cat, he wrapped a hand around the second soldier's mouth and drove the knife down into the side of the man's throat, cutting the jugular vein. Blood squirted like a fountain as he lowered the quivering body to the ground. Hung stood and wiped the blood from his knife as he grinned and held up the decapitated head of the first soldier. The grin faded when the display failed to impress Mattson. Shrugging his shoulders, Hung tossed the head into the brush.

Kendell stood in shock, his mouth still open. It had all happened too fast for him to comprehend. B.J. stepped forward and cut him free. "Who—"

"Keep quiet and stay behind me," whispered Mattson as he turned Kendell around and headed him back in the direction of the plane. At the site, Kendell was panting hard as he said, "I have to stop; I can't go any farther. I need rest."

"Sorry, partner, but we don't have the time. Let's keep it moving," replied B.J. as he signaled two of the bandits to take the point.

Kendell sat down on a nearby rock. Mattson came over and kicked the senator's foot, "I said, not now, mister. Let's move it."

Kendell had just realized that this man was an American soldier. "Do you know who I am?" he asked.

"Buddy, I don't care if you're one of the Pointer Sisters in drag. Get off your ass and let's go."

"Now, just a damn minute! I'll have you know I'm Senator Charles Kendell. If I were you, I'd keep that in mind. I can cause you a lot of trouble when this is over."

"Kendell. I should have known," said B.J. wearily. "Look, I've already got trouble, and as far as that senator shit goes, I'm not impressed. You obviously have me confused with someone who gives a fuck! Now, you stayin' or going with us?" Kendell didn't move.

"Fine by me, Jack," said Mattson as he and Hung took off into the darkness toward the river. Kendell figured the man was bluffing, but what if he wasn't? Forcing himself to his feet, he puffed heavily as he ran to catch up with the two men. He didn't know who this smart ass was, but his career in the military was going to be over as soon as they got back.

Ling slapped the soldier; his excited ranting was making no sense. It worked. Regaining his composure, the soldier slowly explained that the American prisoner was gone and that the two guards had been killed. Ling lost interest in the report when it came to the part of the headless man. Walking away by himself, Ling tried to figure out what was happening here. Kendell was hardly man enough to overpower two of his soldiers, let alone have the guts to kill them. Someone had been at the plane after all. Therefore, it was also possible they had found the money just as Kendell had said. But who? It did not matter. He would have that answer soon enough. Pivoting on his heel, he shouted for two of his best trackers to take the point. They were going after them, no matter who they were. There was that word again: they.

They made it to the river. Mattson put on the headset and began a call-up. "Fox One Alpha, Fox One, over." There was no answer from Ross. He tried Jake. "Fox Two, this is Fox One, over." No answer.

B.J. glanced at his watch. An hour and a half had passed

since they had pulled back from the fortress. Apparently
Ross had taken him at his word and hadn't stopped for
anything. By now they would be making their turn to the
east, away from the river and straight for the Thai border.
He had Kendell, Hung and three bandits; not a formidable
force, but one that should be able to make their way through
this mess without being detected.

Reaching up to remove the headset, B.J. heard a familiar
voice in his earpiece, "Folks One, Folks One, this is Folks
Treee, Folks Treee, Over." B.J. smiled to himself. Fox and
Three were obviously tough words for General San.

"Fox Three, Fox One. I am at the river location. What is
the status on Fox One Alpha and Fox Two? Over."

"Folks One—oh, hell—B.J., they already go. I send half
my men with them, keep half here to wait for you. Good
thing I do this, too." San paused before he said, "You bring
bad company with you."

"What do you mean, Fox Three?"

"Big force, Ling soldiers follow you, behind you right
now. Stay where you at, we cross river farther down, come
up behind them. Folks Threee, good-bye."

Mattson moved back from the river and told Hung to
prepare for action. Kendell was being the usual pain in the
ass. "When are we getting out of here?" he whined.

B.J. leaned forward and placed his hand over the senator's mouth. "You want to get yourself killed, just keep
shootin' off that big mouth. Ling and his boys are trying to
sneak up on us back there, and if I remember right, he's got
a little skinning party planned for you."

Kendell's eyes registered fear. Ling's threat was still very
fresh in his mind.

San's voice came over the radio in a whisper, "B.J., we
cross river. Moving for position. They come for you from
east and south; move slow so you no hear them. You be
ready; fight start, you take man and swim 'cross river. Some
my men there; they help you. Okey, dokey?"

"What about you, General?"

"No worry 'bout me. We wait long time to get Ling in
'nother battle. We no lose this one. Folks Treee, so long."

Mattson looked over at Kendell. "You swim, Senator?"

"Not very well, why?"

"In about one minute all hell is going to break loose, and when it does, you had better be treading water like Mark Spitz, or you'll get your butt shot off. Come on, we're moving down to the edge of the river."

Kendell didn't bother to argue anymore. He'd do as the man said for now. His time would come. He was a very patient man. B.J. freed the pants legs of his jungle fatigues from the top of his boots, wrapped the radio in a waterproof bag, and stuck it into his side pocket. Gunfire suddenly shattered the stillness as muzzle flashes from the two bandits in the rear security positions lit up the night.

"Go, now, Kendell!" yelled B.J. who slid off the bank into the warm water and began swimming for the far bank. Kendell made it as far as his elbows, then stopped. He couldn't do it. He'd never make the distance. A burst of automatic fire snapped in the treetops above his head, causing limbs and leaves to rain down around him. It was just the motivation the man needed; it sent Kendell scrambling off the bank and swimming like the devil was after him.

Midway across, B.J. looked back and saw Kendell was catching up. The jungle was alive with what seemed like a hundred flashes of light as the sound of battle shook the treetops and echoed down the river. The general's men helped them out of the water and moved them back a safe distance from the river. The firefight was at its peak now. San was on the radio again. They were winning the battle. B.J. could see the shadowy figures of Ling and his men silhouetted in the flashes of gunfire. They were being forced back, closer and closer to the river's edge. They would either have to fight to the death or be shot like rats in the water.

Hung heard the sound at the same instant as Mattson. It started like the sound of a large swarm of bees and grew in intensity, louder and louder, as it approached from the north. "Oh, Jesus!" said B.J. as he began to scream into the mike, "San! San, break off the attack! Get out of there! Run, run!"

It was too late. The two Burmese F-one-eleven jet fighters came screaming down from the sky heading straight for the flashes below that served as target beacons for the pilots. Mattson watched helplessly as two teardrop shaped tanks fell, tumbling end over end, from the sky. The jets pulled up and away as the darkness below became a giant fireball turning night into day. The jungle was a roaring inferno as B.J. lowered his head and walked away. Another friend was gone. Hung gave the order and the few remaining bandits fell in behind Mattson and Kendell for the trek down the river to Thailand.

It was morning now. Hung had taken the point for the final leg of the journey to the Thai border. Mattson had not talked to Kendell since the air strike. He preferred to ignore the man's constant complaints and threats. Otherwise he knew he was likely to follow through on the threat Ling had made earlier. He didn't like Kendell and the thought of good men like Lassiter, San, and the American Rangers dying on this trip to save the ungrateful bastard had made the last ten miles seem like an eternity. The only good news had come over the radio at first light when the outpost had reported that Ross and Jake had made it safely across the border with the survivors. Their only encounter was a short exchange of gun fire with a red flag group of Communists who were obviously in need of marksmanship training. One volley from the Rangers had sent them scattering. No one had been hurt. General Johnson and the others were anxiously awaiting his arrival.

Hung raised his hand to halt the group, then he knelt down as B.J. came up beside him and asked, "What's wrong, Hung?"

The bandit's eyes were red; he had been crying. The realization that General San was gone had finally hit home. Pointing across an open plain, he said, "That Thailand. We bandits, we can no go there, Major, but I think you be okay

now. You no need us anymore. We go back and find San.
Take him home to his grandfather. That be okay, Major?"

Mattson didn't know what to say. They owed these
people so much. Then he thought of the money. "Hung,
who has the money?"

"San's grandfather, but no worry; he smart man. He will
see that all people taken care of as his grandson would have
done. We go now, Major. May Buddha smile on you long
time." Hung stood and shook hands with the tall American,
then waved the remnants of a once powerful army back
toward the river and home.

"Where are they going?" asked Kendell in a huffy tone.

"To bury their dead," replied B.J. sadly as he turned and
headed for Thailand. Kendell followed behind.

Jake, General Johnson, Colonel Chakkri, and Lieutenant
Colonel Decker came through the barbed wire in front of the
outpost to greet them. Johnson shook his hand firmly as he
said, "I knew you could do it, B.J. The president and a
grateful congress thank you." At hearing the word president, a beleaguered looking Kendell pushed his way forward.

"What is this about the president? Did he ask about me?
Surely they have made some special arrangements for me,"
said the senator.

"As a matter of fact they have, Senator Kendell. There
are a couple of gentlemen from the State Department
waiting to talk to you in Bangkok. Something about some
numbers they've found that they have traced to a certain
drug dealer in Washington."

Kendell's face went pale. "Why, that's preposterous.
They can't prove a thing."

"I don't know about that, sir. I understand they have a
detailed account of some plan to purchase heroin from a
man in Burma and the sworn statements of two people that
heard you discussing just a plan."

"And just who might these so-called witnesses be?"

"Mrs. Kathryn Nickleson and your wife, sir. Congressman
Nickleson is pressing charges against you for attempted

murder, as well. I have been instructed to see to it that you arrive in Bangkok, sir. I trust I shall not have to place you into custody. Rest assured that nothing would give me greater pleasure. Now, if you'll excuse us, we would like to talk with Major Mattson alone," said Johnson abruptly.

Kendell's eyes showed the look of a broken man as he slowly made his way up the hill to the outpost. "I guess that information we sent you was more valuable than we thought," said Mattson.

"More than you realize, son," replied Johnson. "Once they connected the numbers and the names of Kendell's bodyguards, it led them straight to a major dealer that both the FBI and the DEA had been after for over two years. They busted him last night. The guy was willing to cut a deal; one crooked senator for a reduced sentence. All the lawyers in Washington couldn't get Kendell out of this one."

The thought of Kendell being locked away for twenty to thirty years helped relieve some of the pain B.J. had been carrying. "How are the Nicklesons?" he asked.

"They're doing fine, B.J. All of the survivors are fine. They flew them into Bangkok to the hospital to be checked over as soon as Captain Ross and Jake brought them in. You did a remarkable job, Major."

"Thank you, sir," answered B.J. as he looked around and asked, "Where's General Sweet? I thought he came over with you, sir."

The officers around him began to laugh, Johnson more so than the rest, as he said, "Well, B.J., it seems my deputy fell in with bad company his first hour in town. You see, he wasn't feeling well when we first arrived and wanted to be dropped off at the hotel while I came on up here." Johnson wrinkled an eyebrow to denote he had been suspicious of the action. "Being the concerned commander I am, I had Marshall Parsons contact a friend of his that works with the Thai police to keep an eye on him. Seems General Sweet became a little confused about what you can order from room service and what you do with it once you get it. He denied it, of course, until Marsh's friend showed up this morning with some very impressive pictures that had been taken in an alley behind the hotel. General Sweet is in the Bangkok jail right now, trying to explain the circumstances of his dilemma to the Thai drug enforcement people."

"I'll be damned," laughed B.J. "You mean we're finally going to get that guy out of our hair?"

"Not at all, Major. Colonel Chakkri has informed the police to hold him until we are ready to leave. I don't want him prosecuted. Hell, B.J., if we were to get rid of General Sweet; those assholes on the Hill might replace him with somebody who knows what he's doing."

The group was still laughing at the general's remark as they headed up the hill. As they topped the crest, near the wire, B.J. stopped and turned to stare across at the Burma jungle to bid a final farewell to the friends that had been lost. Johnson told the others to go on, walked up to Mattson and placed his hand on his shoulder. "Never easy is it, son?"

"No, sir. Never."